CREATURE HUNT

by

C.E. Osborn

This is a work of fiction. Names, characters, businesses, places, events and incidents are either the products of the author's imagination or used in a fictitious manner. Any resemblance to actual persons, living or dead, or actual events is purely coincidental.

Cover design:
SelfPubBookCovers.com/LadyLight

© 2019
C.E. Osborn
All rights reserved

For Kris D.

CHAPTER 1

"There's no such thing as Bigfoot."

Zach Larson turned around in surprise. The two men at the table behind him, coffee cups in hand, stared back at him. One of them, gray-haired with a t-shirt, jeans, and a baseball cap, nodded. "Yep. We were talking to you."

"To me?"

"You're the host of that weird-ass show, right? On that so-called documentary channel?"

"Yes, that's me. I'm Zach Larson."

"We know," the other man said. "And I'm telling you again, there's no such thing as Bigfoot."

"I suppose you don't believe in the other monsters we've investigated on the show?" Zach finished his coffee and stood up. He had been in too many of these conversations to want to stick around for the inevitable conclusion.

"Nope," the older man declared. "I've only seen two episodes, but that's enough to know it's utter crap."

"Dad," the younger man interrupted. "You didn't mention you had actually watched it."

"I kept waiting for something to happen." The older man looked up at Zach. "Why not do a show about something real?"

"Many people believe Bigfoot is real," Zach replied patiently. "You gentlemen have a nice day." He nodded at them and left the coffee shop.

Stepping out into the late June sun, Zach blinked and shook his head. Being the host of the show *Creature Hunt* meant that he spent a lot of time in dark places like caves and swamps. He did of lot of work during the night when the subjects of their investigations were supposedly more active.

Western Washington was in a period of beautiful weather. The past week had been clear and in the seventies during the day with cool nights. The nice weather was supposed to continue through the weekend, and as Zach turned to look at Mount Rainier in the distance, he once again marveled at the beauty of the region.

Two years ago, at the age of twenty-nine, Zach had been working as a writer for a textbook company. One of his co-workers, knowing that Zach was skeptical about creatures like Bigfoot, had heard that there were auditions being held for a reality television show and suggested that Zach submit a tape. Zach had looked over the requirements for the show and had traveled to a large lake in search of a monster that was said to cruise its depths. The tape had included an encounter with some of the local people attempting to protect the legendary creature.

To his surprise, he had been selected from thousands of audition tapes for what the producers of the show had called his "quiet reassurance" during the investigation. Since then, his life had involved a lot of travel, a lot of research, and interviews with what seemed like an endless supply of like-minded people. Those witnesses who had always seemed skeptical of what they had seen were the ones that most interested him. He was beginning to become tired of people who insisted that every crack of a branch or unusual howl in a forest was a werewolf, goat man, or Bigfoot.

Creature Hunt was on a break for a few months while the producers decided what to look for next. The break had not come soon enough for Zach, as they had just finished filming the second season. He had walked into his house late last night and flopped down on the bed, almost instantly falling asleep with the window open and the refreshing air blowing over him.

"I need a vacation," Zach murmured to himself as he reached his house. He turned around again and eyed Mount Rainier.

An idea formed in his head. He had once driven by a group of cabins on his way to the mountain. He recalled that they were just a few miles from the park border. Letting himself into the house, he rushed to his computer. A search led him to the website for Mitzi's Cabin Resort. He looked at the options and found that a small cabin next to a creek was still available.

It was Wednesday. Zach decided to head out tomorrow for a long weekend of relaxation. Once the reservation was e-mailed to him, he printed it out and ran up to his bedroom to start packing. He filled his bag with sweatpants and short-sleeved shirts, jeans and a couple of hooded sweatshirts. All the clothes he owned with the *Creature* Hunt logo had been washed this morning and relegated to their reserved dresser drawer.

At the last minute, he decided to take his backpack filled with his personal investigation gear. He hadn't even bothered to look through it and unpack it yet, so he'd make time for that during the weekend. He already knew that the notebooks from his last few investigations were still inside.

The cabin had most of the amenities he needed, but he'd have to stop and buy groceries on the way. As he placed clothes in his suitcase, Zach felt his mood lifting. Five months of hotel living and occasional check-ins with one of his friends to make sure his house was still standing had started to get on his nerves recently. He had been happy when the producers had called him to let him know that they needed to take a break before the third season. Ratings were high, and fans of the show had been sending numerous suggestions for different monsters and locations to be investigated.

There was one person he wanted to talk to before he left on vacation. One of his cameramen, Brandon, lived in Oregon and had already embarked on another project during the break. Zach dialed his number and smiled as Brandon answered. "Zach! Did you find the Loch Ness monster yet?"

"Come on, Brandon. Would I look for that without you?"

"Given what we've caught on camera together, I think you'd have better luck alone," Brandon retorted. "Except for finding the Jersey Devil, of course." They both fell silent, remembering what had happened on that investigation back in March. "Anyway, what's up?"

"Just wanted to let you know that I'm heading out to

Mount Rainier for a few days of vacation."

There was silence on the other end. "You didn't hear the latest?" Brandon asked.

"No. What happened?"

"There have been some Bigfoot sightings near the mountain in the past couple of weeks. I wouldn't be surprised if you run into a group of people roaming around looking for footprints and banging on trees."

Zach groaned. The crew had been in California a couple of months ago looking for Bigfoot and he remembered the types of people he had encountered. "Well, I'll do my best to avoid them. I'm just going to hang out in my cabin, maybe go for a hike, and explore some of the scenery out there."

"Have a nice time," Brandon said with a laugh. "Bring a Bigfoot back for me."

Zach laughed and they chatted for a few minutes before ending the call. He stretched and brought his bags down to the living room, then ordered Chinese food for dinner. By the time his sesame chicken arrived, he had turned off his computer and his phone and was watching a baseball game. When he went to bed hours later, he smiled at the prospect of a few days away from hunting monsters.

CHAPTER 2

Autumn Hunter walked in her front door and slammed it behind her. She instantly felt guilty as she saw her cat scamper out of the living room and up the stairs. "Sorry!" she called out as his tail disappeared from sight.

She tossed her purse on the chair and groaned as she sank down on the couch. It had been a busy day at work, followed by one of the worst dates she had ever experienced. She shook her head as she thought back to when she had first arrived at the restaurant.

"You look just like your photos," Nick had said, obviously surprised.

Autumn had looked at him and nodded, biting her lip. His description of "slightly receding hairline" was actually "mostly bald." His listed height of six feet tall was nearly six inches shorter than advertised, and at no point during their recent communications had he mentioned that he was currently recovering from an allergic reaction that left a bright red rash all over his arms.

Still, she had given him a chance and tried to enjoy the evening. As they were leaving the restaurant, Nick had dropped two bombshells. "You're too fat for me," he had said. "I don't think it's worth leaving my wife for you."

Now, Autumn tried to smile as she ran a hand across her stomach. Yes, she was about thirty pounds over her ideal weight, a fact which was very obvious in several places on her profile. She wondered why she had bothered being honest. This was the third date in a row where the man in question had lied on at least two parts of his profile.

Trying to shake off the evening, Autumn went over to her desk in the corner of the living room. The Bigfoot Online Group message board had been more active than usual lately. She wanted to check in and see the latest updates.

Her cat, Squatch, came back down the stairs and sat by her chair, staring pointedly at Autumn until she patted her leg. He jumped up and sat down, purring as her attention remained fixed on the screen. She started to pet him, her eyes wide as she read some of the posts.

Her phone rang and she checked the caller's name. "Hi, Erica," she answered. "Have you read the latest on the BOG?"

"Yep. A few of us are getting ready to head out to Mount Rainier this weekend."

"Who's going?" Autumn switched over to her calendar.

"The usual team. Me, Tiffany, Mike, Nate, and Bill," Erica replied. "They're planning to set up the RV and a tent at the campground. I, on the other hand, have rented a cabin at Mitzi's Cabin Resort."

"Anyone staying with you?"

"Nope. That's why I called you. I'm sure the campers will have a few more people joining them, so I wanted to give you a chance to stay with me."

Autumn looked at her work schedule. "I'm working a half day at the library tomorrow morning, but I'll be done at noon. I can pack tonight and join you in time for dinner."

"Can you stay all weekend?"

"Yep! I've had a lot of overtime lately and they told me to take some time off."

"Sweet! We can get dinner somewhere before we arrive at the cabin."

"See you tomorrow, Erica."

"Bye!"

Autumn smiled, feeling much better. She was convinced that one day BOG would find evidence of Bigfoot. She truly believed that it existed, and she longed to prove that everyone who had had an experience with the monster was right, and that people would finally believe them.

"I'm going away for a few days," she told Squatch. "I'll call my parents to have them come check on you and feed you." He yawned and jumped down, allowing her to go upstairs and start packing.

She turned on the television in her room and saw that there was a *Creature Hunt* marathon going on. She paused, a sweatshirt in her hand, as Zach Larson prowled the shores of Lake Champlain in New York. He was looking for the famed lake monster.

Since starting to watch the show, she had developed a small crush on the handsome host. This had been one of the first episodes, and she had been an avid fan since the start. Given that the show was on a prominent network, she hoped that people who had never taken an interest in cryptozoology were starting to do their own research.

Autumn's own interest dated back to her freshman year of high school. She had gone to the school library after walking past a group of senior guys making fun of her and had sat down in a deserted section. After a few minutes of silent tears, she had looked up at the shelves and seen a book about Bigfoot.

Growing up in the Pacific Northwest, Autumn had heard stories about Bigfoot for most of her life. They had come in the form of urban legends, with the story almost always happening to someone's best friend's college roommate's brother. She had laughed them off, but that day in the library she reached out for the book and looked through it. She was intrigued by the illustrations and looked up and down the shelves for books on other legends. She had brought home six books that day and her interest had grown.

Now, ten years later at twenty-five years old, she was a library assistant and hid a smile when people came in to ask, always with a tentative look in their eyes, if she knew where they could find information about Bigfoot. Or the Loch Ness monster. Or werewolves, or any other assortment of odd creatures. She never laughed at them, because she knew firsthand what that felt like on the receiving end.

"I wonder if I'll ever meet him in person," she said out loud, her eyes turning back to Zach Larson. She also wondered if he actually believed in the monsters he was looking for. She shrugged, turning her attention to preparing for a weekend of hunting for Bigfoot.

CHAPTER 3

Tahoma Valley, just to the west of Mount Rainier National Park, was a small town with several stores that catered to tourists. People drove through on their way to and from the mountain and bought picnic food and drinks, filled their coolers with ice, purchased cheap sweatshirts and t-shirts, and sometimes stayed for a drink at the Valley Tavern. Souvenir shops sold everything from local Native American art to candy. There were several businesses in the few strip malls along the town that mostly catered to locals, but overall the sense of Tahoma Valley was that people were just passing through on their way to more interesting places.

On this Wednesday night, Mitzi Taylor was wandering through her resort. She only had two out of ten cabins occupied tonight. The others would be filled tomorrow and Friday and she was booked solid through the weekend. Once July arrived in a couple of weeks, the resort would be full every week until Labor Day. This time of year was a busy one for her and her husband Marvin, and more than made up for some of the slower winter months.

She had deliberately set up the resort so that each cabin only had one neighbor. The five groups made a nice circle around the general store and office where Marvin and a couple of local teenagers worked. The sign out on the highway was lit for the evening with bold green and blue, with the resort logo of a miniature cabin outlined in brown. It was a quiet evening, and the sunset was bringing darkness to the resort.

Mitzi stopped when she reached the clearing that housed Cabin 1 and Cabin 2. These would both be occupied tomorrow night. The last reservation for the weekend had come in just a couple of hours earlier. Tomorrow she'd come back here and make sure the linens were fresh and the cabins had been tidied. She provided most of the amenities to make the stay easier for people who wanted to say they were camping but still wanted to have four walls around them. She understood that feeling, especially living out here.

She walked around Cabin 1 and stopped at the creek that ran past her property. It was only a few feet wide and easy enough to cross, but she still warned most people to stay away from it. There was a lake on the other side of town as well as rivers and creeks closer to the mountain that could be explored. Most guests heeded her warning, since the creek was only accessible next to this cabin and Cabin 4, a few hundred yards away and hidden from view by a stand of trees and high bushes.

She saw the structure and noted that it was still standing. The last time a shelter like this had been built using downed tree limbs and nearby boulders, it had taken six men from town almost an entire day to tear down the structure that had been built up overnight. Now, another one was in its place. Mitzi didn't like the sight of it. She felt it would only bring trouble close to her home.

A hand on her shoulder made her turn around in fright. She calmed down when she saw Stan Smith, a retired police officer, and her husband Marvin. They had walked up silently behind her. "Hi, Mitzi," Marvin said, taking her hand. "I thought you were probably out this way."

"I check on that place every now and then," Mitzi replied. "Hi, Stan. What brings you up this way?"

"Just thought I'd come by and let you know that George's truck was broken into this morning." George was one of Stan's sons, a utility worker for the county. His other son, Carson, ran a medical clinic in town. "He thinks whoever it was smelled the fish he had caught the day before and was trying to take some."

You mean *what*ever it was," Marvin corrected him. "We all know that no one's going to walk up to a truck in someone's driveway because they think they smell fish."

"Deputy Singleton said it might be a hermit living off the land looking for an easy score," Stan replied with a shake of his head.

"Joey has been here three years and should know better by

now," Mitzi said. "She's always looking for a reason other than the obvious one."

"I see they've been over here," Marvin said softly, looking across the creek.

Stan nodded. "Reilly said he was out here this morning and saw it. I guess he's advising Carson and the others to leave it up for now."

"I have guests staying in these cabins this weekend," Mitzi replied sharply. "I don't know if it's a good idea for them to see that."

All three of them looked at the structure again. There was no movement that they could see other than some stray leaves blowing in the evening breeze. Mitzi suddenly shivered and Marvin put his arm around her. She turned away from the creek and they started walking back to the general store.

"The campgrounds on both sides of town are full," Stan said. "I guess a lot of Bigfoot hunters are descending on Tahoma Valley this weekend."

"Damn," Marvin swore. "Let me guess. A couple of people thought they saw a Bigfoot wandering in the forest and posted about it online. That's how those nuts always get it in their head to come out here."

"It's a popular area for people thinking they see Bigfoot," Stan replied calmly. "You know that."

Mitzi and Marvin nodded. A lot of sightings occurred in and around the mountain and surrounding park and towns. People had sometimes stopped at the resort just to ask the employees if they had seen something. The Bigfoot hunters were always prepared with their cameras and recorders, some going low-tech with notebooks and pens. Mitzi usually ended up selling them some food to supposedly attract the creature along with some type of Bigfoot souvenir from the area dedicated to the legend at the back of the store. Those who stopped by on their way in had rarely come back to report on anything they had found.

Hopefully this weekend would be the same. Mitzi doubted

that most of her guests would be interested in Bigfoot. The two outliers might be those staying in the cabins near the creek. One of them had mentioned being part of the Bigfoot Online Group.

She was pulled from her thoughts by Stan opening his car door. "How's George doing these days?" she asked him. "Has he seen anything else recently?"

Stan shrugged. "He doesn't usually tell me or Carson unless it's something physical, like the truck." He shook his head. "Maybe I'll keep a closer eye on him this weekend. It's the anniversary, you know."

Mitzi and Marvin nodded grimly. One of the local teens had been killed in a mysterious accident ten years ago. Most people in the community remembered it and tried to steer visitors away from the area where it had happened in order to avoid a repetition of the incident. Mitzi and Marvin, who were close friends with Stan, were among the few who knew the truth behind the death.

Stan drove away, waving his hand. Marvin went back into the store, where he would remain until it was time to close the gates for the evening. Mitzi went behind the office and followed the clearly marked path down to their house. It was the same size as their largest cabin and very comfortable. She settled in to watch a movie and tried to keep her mind off of the shelter across the creek.

Two miles away, George Smith sat in his living room drinking a can of beer. He had called the police to report the broken window and Deputy Singleton had come out to take a look. He was sure she would never figure out what had happened, but had let her take pictures and fill out the paperwork. It wasn't the first time that something had happened to his truck or house, and it wouldn't be the last.

He emptied the can and went into the kitchen for another one. It was ten years since his friend Harry had died. The first couple of years after the incident had been rough. George had gone from job to job, not finding anything he wanted to do with his life. Reilly had finally suggested that he get some training at a technical college away from Tahoma Valley. George had moved away for two years and returned with a job working the utility lines out in this region of the county. It was fulfilling work for him and left him plenty of time to fish or hang out with his friends at the tavern.

The secret that he carried with him, though, had returned to stalk him once he had moved back into town. Even living in a different house didn't help. He still often felt he was being watched and would see a dark face and rage-filled eyes looking in the window at him some evenings. The monster always left when it knew George had seen it. And it was always the same creature. George could identify it by the color of its hair and a scar on its body.

It was almost impossible for him to date anyone, although he occasionally went out with his friends and their wives. He didn't want to bring a woman back here because of what she might see some night. Even when he had lived in the city, he would be on the lookout for that face and those eyes whenever he invited someone over to his apartment.

There was a waitress at the tavern that he had become interested in, and he hoped from the way she talked to him that she was interested too. Having grown up here, he knew she had heard stories of Bigfoot. He thought that she might possibly be one of the few people who would understand if he explained what haunted him.

Most of the stores in the strip mall had closed by the time Deputy Reilly Brown pulled into the parking lot. He ignored the people gathered near some cars by the grocery store, knowing they were teenagers talking and making plans for the weekend. If they were still hanging out when Joey came through here on patrol later, she'd chat with them to make sure nothing illegal was happening.

Reilly knocked on the door of the medical clinic. Although there were official business hours posted on the door, he knew that Carson Smith often stayed late in case an emergency came in. The doctor appeared at the end of the hallway and walked down to let Reilly in. His gait was unhurried and steady, almost the exact opposite of his brother. Unless George was at work and needed to be slow and careful, he always seemed to be in a hurry to get from one place to another.

"Hi, Reilly. What's up?" Carson asked when the deputy entered the clinic.

"Anyone else here?"

"No, I sent the nurses home for the night. One of them is on call in case something happens." Carson led Reilly back to the kitchenette and both men found cans of soda in the refrigerator. "So, what brings you here tonight?"

"I've already seen a couple of groups arriving here in town because of increased Bigfoot sighting reports."

Carson swore. "You think they'll be in danger?"

"I think we're going to have to be vigilant this weekend. I don't know who's had those sightings because I don't read that online forum most of them follow."

"I'd be willing to bet that most of the sightings were real this time," Carson said. "It's that time of year, you know."

Reilly sighed. "Yeah, I know. And there's been another tree shelter built by Mitzi's place."

"Let me and the others get rid of it."

"Not this time."

"Why not, Reilly?"

"If we're going to have people looking for Bigfoot around here, then it would be better for them to find someplace they think it lives than for them to go where it actually lives."

"Mitzi won't be happy."

"No, and I'm not thrilled with it either. But let those people go crazy with their photos and their speculations about what built it. Don't add anything to the structure, just let it be. If they're busy in one place, we can keep a better eye on them."

"Where do the Bigfoot people usually start their searches?"

"At the opposite end of the trail leading to the structure."

"I'll get some guys together to try to discourage them from heading further down that path than necessary."

"Nothing physical," Reilly warned. He knew the guys Carson was talking about. They were nice men, but very protective of the secrets of the town and surrounding forest. Dwayne, Todd, and Luke had often been asked in the past to step in when some Bigfoot hunters got a little too ambitious about where they looked for the creature.

"Of course not," Carson said with a pained expression. "We've never had to hurt someone. Sometimes suggestion works better than you might think. Especially when you can convince someone hunting for a legend that the legend actually exists somewhere."

Reilly nodded. "Okay. I guess more people will be in town tomorrow. Take care, Carson."

He left the clinic and drove home. On the way, he saw a few trucks leaving the Valley Tavern and decided to let Joey and the other deputy on duty tonight handle them. He needed some rest before Tahoma Valley was filled with people on their quest to find Bigfoot.

CHAPTER 4

When Zach set out for Mount Rainier the next morning, he looked at his investigation equipment again before finally deciding to bring it along. Brandon had mentioned that there had been some Bigfoot sightings recently. Although he was trying to take a break, he still wanted to be prepared. If he really could catch some evidence of Bigfoot on camera, or even get some sound recordings, that would be a great boost for the show.

Zach drove leisurely once he got off the highway. He stopped at a small grocery store and bought several food and drink items for the cabin, placing them in the small cooler in his backseat. The cabins were only a few minutes away, but he decided to stop in town before heading over to the resort. The large sign in front of the Valley Tavern proclaimed the establishment to be open for lunch, so he pulled into the lot and decided to give it a chance.

When he walked in, he instantly knew that people had already labeled him as a stranger. There were several pool tables in the back of a large room off to the right. Men were gathered around a couple of them, and his entrance made them stop their games and turn to look. They were similarly dressed in different versions of jeans, flannel shirts, and t-shirts. A bar took up space in the near area of the game room, and while no one was seated at the stools around it a bartender was still on duty. Zach assumed he had probably served the men playing pool the beer bottles they were holding.

A hallway in front of him contained the entrance and waiting area where he now stood, along with the restrooms and a vending machine. An equally large room off to his left appeared to be the main dining room. Here, the environment was one of a cozy log cabin. A waitress dressed in jeans and a plaid shirt walked up to him as he turned in that direction.
"Hello, sir. Table for one?"
"Yes, please."

"Right this way." She led him to a booth along the wall that separated the dining room from the hallway. "My name is Jessie and I'll be taking care of you. Can I get you something to drink?"

"Can I just have a diet pop?"

"Sure." She left a menu on his table and started back towards the kitchen. "George, get back over to the bar and finish your game."

Zach looked up to see that one of the men from the other room had come over and was looking in his direction. He smiled and nodded, then kept his head down as he perused the menu. Out of the corner of his eye he saw the man leave. Jessie reappeared with his drink.

"Thanks. Who was that man?"

"Oh, just one of several local men who come here to drink and play pool. They'll leave soon to go back to wherever they need to be, and then most of them will come back later tonight if they don't have wives or families."

"They drink before going back to work?"

Jessie frowned. "Depends on their job. You probably saw several beer bottles, but a lot of them also drink water. They just like to gather here and shoot some pool."

Zach smiled. "I'll have the club sandwich with fries, please."

Jessie smiled back. "Good choice."

She took the menu, seated a family of four that had appeared in the doorway, and headed back to the kitchen. Zach stood and wandered over to an area of wall that had been decorated with several pictures. There were also short snippets of stories to go along with some of the photos.

One story was about a man who had died in the area ten years ago. Harry Pike had apparently been injured while hiking in the woods with his friend, George Smith. The police were still looking into the matter.

Zach wondered if they had ever found anything suspicious about the death. Another picture caught his eye. It was a man standing next to a large footprint. "Local man George Smith supposedly found evidence of Bigfoot," the story read. "George claims it must be a hoax."

Zach recognized the man who had come into the restaurant to stare at him. He looked at the other pictures and returned to his booth just as Jessie brought his food over to him. He was enjoying his sandwich when suddenly George returned and, without asking, sat down across from him.

"I recognize you," he said quietly. "You're that guy from the show about monsters."

"Yes," Zach said just as quietly. "I'm here on vacation."

"You'd be better off not being here at all, at least not this weekend," George said. "Some people around here having been getting crazed up over supposed Bigfoot sightings."

"I saw your picture on the wall," Zach said. "Do you think that footprint was a hoax?"

"Doesn't matter what I think, what matters is what's real. If you're here on vacation, enjoy your stay. If you're here to try to prove to the world that Bigfoot exists, you'd better turn away now." George saw Jessie coming over and quickly exited.

"How's everything, sir?"

"Fine," he said. "Just having a quick chat with George."

"Hopefully he wasn't his usual grumpy self."

"No, not really," Zach replied thoughtfully. He finished his meal and paid, noting as he left that the dining room was now half-full and another waitress was on duty. The bar remained empty except for the pool players. George glanced up as Zach left, but didn't acknowledge him in any way.

"Now that was interesting," Zach said out loud as he got back into his car. He drove to Mitzi's Cabin Resort and looked around before going to the main cabin to check in. A map showed that there were ten cabins, each in groups of two branching off from the gravel road through the resort. There was also a convenience store and gift shop. He wasn't surprised to see the typical section of Bigfoot items inside. Books by scientists in the field, carvings, plush animals, and bright shirts all celebrated the mysterious creature.

Zach went over to the front cabin and entered. Behind a desk, a middle-aged woman stood up and smiled. "Hi! How can I help you today?"

"My name is Zach Larson. I reserved a cabin for the weekend."

The woman checked a sheet in front of her and nodded. "I have you in Cabin 1, just down the road and to the right. You'll have neighbors in Cabin 2 arriving later tonight."

"Sounds fine."

"I just need your credit card."

Zach went through the routine of checking in. After giving her his credit card, driver's license, and phone number, he was given two keys for the cabin. "There's a creek behind your cabin," Mitzi advised. "I wouldn't go wading or anything, though. The lake is five miles down the highway if you want to go swimming or boating."

"Thanks. Do you have a lot of people this weekend?"

"We're full. The camping area down the highway is also full. I guess that's not unusual for a June weekend. People want to get out here while the weather is nice." She pointed to a white board on the wall where someone had written out the forecast for the next five days, along with today's current weather. "Still cool at night, especially up here, but the days are nice."

"Yes, they are." Zach smiled at Mitzi. "Are the gates open late?"

"Until midnight. Then my husband closes them and if someone wants to come in, they need to push the buzzer and enter the code on the back of the key envelope there." Zach turned it over and indeed found a four-digit code. "Doesn't happen often. After a day exploring around the mountain people are usually grateful to get back here in time to have dinner and lounge around the cabins."

"Anything unusual going on around here?" Zach asked casually. Mitzi frowned.

"I heard there was some people from a Bigfoot online forum in the area. I guess they think they'll find the monster this time. People have told me someone they know once thought they saw Bigfoot. You know how stories like that usually go."

Zach did know, all too well. There were a lot of stories he had listened to for *Creature Hunt* that had started with "My best friend's sister's boyfriend..." and he had always viewed those stories with doubt. He was more interested in talking to the actual eyewitnesses.

"Well, thanks. I'll probably stop by sometime during the weekend."

"The convenience store and gift shop are open from seven in the morning until ten at night.," Mitzi replied. "Show your key and you can get one free bottle of soda each day."

Zach smiled and drove down to his cabin. It was easy to find. It was an A-frame design with a long porch along the front with two chairs on it, three steps leading up to the front door. Inside, he saw that the bedroom was a loft overlooking the cozy main floor. He stepped into a living room that contained a couch and recliner, and also a large television. The kitchen was also on the main floor along with a small dining nook. There was a half bath down on this level also.

He left his luggage and cooler in the living room and climbed the stairs to the loft. There was a full bathroom with a shower up here, and a king-size bed. Two windows overlooked the creek out back. The decorations were all in dark greens and blues, and he found the atmosphere to be cozy. It was very relaxing. After he unpacked his clothes and the food, he settled down onto the couch and closed his eyes for a rare midday nap.

CHAPTER 5

Autumn got off to a later start than she had planned. A problem had occurred with the online catalog at work and she had been asked to solve it, which she had done with almost no effort. The person who had caused the problem had done it before, and it was not the first time that Autumn's knowledge of the system had restored the database to successful operation.

Then, she had decided on the spur of the moment to get her hair cut before leaving town. She had ignored her light red hair for a long time because she did not enjoy sitting in the salon chair while the stylist chatted with her. Today had been busy in the salon, though, so she was able to get about three inches cut off without much conversation. When she got home, she brushed out her hair and was pleased with how much more vibrant it seemed.

She had also stopped at a drugstore to get a pack of gum and a soda to settle her stomach while driving up parts of the mountain highway and to buy a bottle of body wash. She had realized on her way out of the driveway that she had forgotten hers inside and decided to just get a new one. She had smelled several of the options and found a nice vanilla scent.

She found the campground where Tiffany, Nate, Mike, and Bill were staying. Mike and Bill were cousins, and Tiffany and Nate were close friends of Autumn's. She had known Nate first. When he had met Tiffany, she had first formed an unfavorable impression when Tiffany openly questioned Nate's hobby. Now, Tiffany was actively involved most of the times when they went out here for the weekend. She wasn't on the BOG forum much, but Autumn was glad that at least she was willing to be open-minded about Bigfoot.

Nate owned an RV, and he and Tiffany had parked it about midway down a row filled with other campers. Mike and Bill had set up a tent on the same site, although Autumn knew that they would probably also be sleeping in the RV. When she pulled up into the bit of extra space allowed by the huge vehicle, Tiffany saw her from inside and waved, then said something to a person behind her. Nate opened the door and smiled.

"Autumn! Glad you're here! Tiffany gave Erica a ride down. Hopefully you can bring her back on Sunday."

"Of course!" She hugged Nate. "I'm hungry. What are the plans for dinner?"

"Mike and Bill are working on a stir-fry inside. We thought we'd go to the ice cream store in town for dessert. It's open late and we haven't really had a chance to see the local area. This is the first time I've investigated in Tahoma Valley."

"Me, too," Autumn admitted. "It seems like this spot has become much more active in recent years."

"Well, come inside," Nate urged. Autumn stepped around him and greeted everyone. Tiffany and Erica were already seated at the dinette with plates on the table. Erica had her laptop out and was showing something to Tiffany. Mike and Bill were in the kitchenette. Bill's huge stature made him hard to miss, and a tight squeeze for the RV, but he always found a way to make Autumn feel good on these trips. He was always ready with a well-timed joke or compliment. Mike was shorter than his cousin, and a little more serious-minded, but he was always pleasant and Autumn was comfortable around both of them.

"Hi, Autumn!" they called in unison. Erica gestured to her laptop.

"There are lots of reports coming from this stretch of the highway. Someone already claimed to have actually seen a Bigfoot killing a deer."

"I don't think I believe that," Nate said, joining the women at the table. "At least not in plain view."

"Maybe he didn't know he was being seen," Tiffany suggested. "Or maybe it was a deer carcass, killed on the road, and Bigfoot was just bringing it back to his home."

"I think that's far more likely," Autumn said. The dinette was just large enough for her to join the others. She looked at the screen in front of Erica. "And that's one of the lousiest pictures I've seen."

Erica shook her head. "I know. I just don't get it. Why can't anyone who has these encounters get a good picture?"

"You were hiking one of the trails up here last summer," Bill pointed out, stirring something in a pan. "You saw a deer and by the time you got your camera out and ready, it was gone. Most of these are likely surprise encounters, and people don't always have the equipment available to get a shot in time."

"I have a good feeling about this weekend," Mike said. He and Bill brought dinner to the table and they all served themselves. "With all the live reports coming in, I'm surprised we were able to find a spot here."

"Is there anything going on in town this weekend?" Nate asked. "Any local festivals in the area?"

"I didn't see any signs for something like that when I stopped at the grocery store," Bill replied. "That was the first thought I had, actually. That maybe there was something else going on in the area and the locals thought the best way to promote it was to list a bunch of potentially promising Bigfoot sightings on the internet."

"You'd think that would have the opposite effect on most people they'd want to attract to those festivals," Tiffany argued. "Like the Tahoma Days festival in August. Most parents aren't going to want to bring their kids to a place where a huge monster might be lurking just off every trail."

"I agree," Autumn said. "Most locals would want to downplay any sighting of Bigfoot even at the quietest times of year. I doubt they'd be hyping it up themselves."

"When are we going to do our first investigation?" Erica said, finally putting her computer away. She had waited until everyone else was eating and finally put some of the stir-fry on her plate. "There are some BOG members on the other side of town camping near the lake and they invited us to join them tomorrow around eleven."

"I hear Tony Simons is in the area this weekend," Mike said. "Hopefully we won't run into him."

All the team members nodded. They had a bad history with a couple of other teams from previous searches. Tony Simons led one of them. Most of the rest of his team were decent people. Tony, though, enjoyed taking credit for anything discovered by other BOG members.

"That sounds good," Nate said. "That will let you and Autumn get settled in to your cabin tonight."

"Yep," Autumn agreed. She thought about the newly acquired field manual out in her car. "I have a new notebook for this investigation. Hopefully we can fill it up this time. The last investigation didn't provide us with much of anything."

"As I recall, Bill came up with some photos of what turned out to be his reflection," Mike chuckled. "Better make sure you wear that neon coat this weekend, cousin."

"Oh, I will," Bill assured him.

They laughed and joked with each other through dinner, and after the dishes had been cleaned up they set out for the ice cream shop. As she drove down the highway through the town of Tahoma Valley, Autumn noticed that a lot of people were out on this summer evening. When she and Erica pulled into the store's parking lot behind Nate's car, there were only a few spots still available.

The ice cream shop was at one end of the largest strip mall in town. Many people had come here for the choice of the ice cream shop, a chain fast food restaurant, a drugstore, a take-out pizza place, a coffee shop that had already closed for the evening, and a family-style restaurant at the far end. There was a bank in the parking lot, and the grocery store across the street seemed to be doing a brisk business.

The team entered the ice cream shop. There were several empty tables, and Tiffany and Mike went to claim one while the others placed their orders. Autumn was happy to see that they had both mint chocolate chip and peppermint ice cream, and she bought a bowl with a scoop of each.

When the group was finally settled down and enjoying their treats, the door opened and several young men, dressed as if they had spent the day working in the outdoors, entered. They looked around and when their gaze fell on the BOG group, a couple of them gestured and said something to their friends. They ordered their ice cream and sat down at a nearby table.

One of the strangers smiled grimly at them. "I haven't seen any of you around town before. I'm guessing you're here because you think you'll find Bigfoot."

"That's right," Nate said, meeting the man's gaze. "Seen him around?"

The other man laughed, but to Autumn's relief it was accompanied with a pleasant smile. "Nah. But we have seen other people out there today. Just be careful where you're going in the forest. We had to help someone who nearly sprained their ankle trying to get down a hill."

Mike asked a question, and soon the local men were talking to the BOG group about weather conditions and forest undergrowth. Autumn knew those would be important, but she just focused on her ice cream and glanced at Erica. She knew her friend was probably bored. They couldn't wait to get to their cabin, get some sleep, and be able to start a new investigation the next day.

Zach walked out onto the cabin porch and sat down. Other than the light next to the front door, darkness surrounded him. Mitzi had told him that the cabin across from his would be occupied later tonight. For now, he was going to enjoy the peace.

The creek behind the cabin made soft splashing noises as the water ran over a series of rocks. There was a gentle wind that barely disturbed the branches of the giant pine trees surrounding the cabins. And from somewhere nearby, the sound of heavy breathing drifted through the foliage.

Zach's senses came alive. Instincts from his on-camera

investigations kicked in, and he quietly looked in the direction of the gravel road that came in from the main highway. He could see nothing, but he knew that he had heard the breathing. An animal was around here somewhere.

He felt a shiver down his back. Standing up, he took a couple steps down and left the porch, walking towards the road. He wished he had brought his flashlight outside and for a moment he considered going back inside to get it. He was clearly visible to anyone, or anything, that was looking his way.

He heard a low growl come from the trees beyond the second cabin. Shaking his head, he quietly retreated inside his cabin and turned off the porch light. Shutting the solid wood door, he locked it and placed the chain in place. Keeping all the lights off, Zach sat down on the couch next to the window and waited for several minutes.

No one emerged from the forest. "Damn," Zach swore, and turned on the lights. He pulled the curtains across the windows and decided to ignore what he had just experienced. He was trying to get away from his constant immersion into cryptozoology, not go out seeking something he didn't know if he wanted to find. Turning on the television, he pulled a beer out of the fridge and settled down to watch several episodes of an older comedy show that he still enjoyed.

His channel flipping landed on *Creature Hunt* just as a new episode was airing. There were two more episodes left after this in the current season. He saw the words Jersey Devil flash across the screen and shuddered. That had been a dark investigation, both because they were investigating in New Jersey during March and because of what they seen but been unable to catch on camera. The creature had touched them both physically and mentally. He shook his head and changed to something else.

Two hours later, Zach looked out the window. Something large and dark ran across the road, from one stand of thick trees to another. Sitting up, he turned off the television and stared outside again. The night remained still, but this time he thought he could make out someone standing near the other cabin. He got up and rummaged through his backpack for his flashlight and camera, turned off the inside lights, and once again stepped out on the porch.

With no light behind him, Zach carefully walked to where he had first seen the dark shape emerge from the forest. "I wish you were here, Brandon," he muttered, and then took a couple of quick pictures. Tree branches shook on the other side of the road, behind Cabin 2. Zach turned on his flashlight and shined it right in the forest.

"Who's there?" he called out. No response came.

"I'm going back inside and calling the police," he said, starting to back away from the woods. "This is your last chance."

"Wait," a voice replied. Two people emerged from the forest, a tall man and a medium-height woman, looking sheepish. They were dressed in dark green and brown clothing and held flashlights and cameras of their own.

"Who are you and what are you doing here?" he asked, his voice filled with both relief and anger.

"I'm Nate and this is Tiffany. We're camping just down the highway. We have two friends staying in this other cabin this weekend. They must have stopped on their way in from town. When we realized they weren't here yet, we decided to look around in the forest."

"What are you looking for?"

"Bigfoot," the man replied promptly. Zach sighed. The woman looked down at the ground, but he could see a hint of a smile on her face.

"Really?"

The man's mouth suddenly opened in recognition. Zach knew exactly what was coming next. "Oh my God! You're Zach Larson, the host of *Creature Hunt*!"

The woman shrieked in surprise. "You are! You must be here for our hunt this weekend!"

Zach shook his head. "Sorry. I'm on vacation at the moment. Have a good night." Smiling at the strangers, he turned and walked back to the cabin. It was nearly ten o'clock, and time for him to get into bed and relax. Before closing the door, he saw the man and woman setting out down the road, their flashlights occasionally being directed towards the heavy foliage on each side of the road.

He now knew what his neighbors would be doing this weekend. He wondered if they would also be sneaking around in the forest at night. If so, he'd ask them to at least warn him so he didn't get nervous at every movement between the trees.

Zach yawned and locked the door again. He went into the kitchen for a cold bottle of water, then turned out the lights on the lower level and climbed up to the loft. He crawled between the sheets and pulled the warm plaid comforter over him. He read a mystery novel for about thirty minutes, realizing how quiet it was outside except for the sounds of the creek. Just before he fell asleep, he heard the sound of a car coming down the gravel road and two female voices outside the cabin.

Business was light at the Valley Tavern on Thursday night. In the bar, Jessie had come in after her shift and changed one of the television sets to watch *Creature Hunt*. The rest of the room was immersed in playing pool or watching baseball. Troy, the night bartender, brought Jessie her dinner and motioned to the show she was watching.

"A bunch of idiots like those people that blond guy is interviewing are already here in town," he said.

"I know," she replied. "And so is that blond guy. I served him at lunch today."

Two deputies walked in. They often came by the Valley Tavern on their patrol to check in and make sure no one was getting out of line. The few locals that got drunk from time to time were seldom foolish enough to get behind the wheel and drive home, since they never knew when the police would be around. Troy was glad for their presence.

"Hi, Reilly. Hi, Joey."

The man and woman nodded and took seats at the bar. Troy offered them glasses of water, which they both received with a smile. "Anything different tonight?" Joey asked. She had been on patrol in Tahoma Valley for nearly three years now. She knew that June often brought an influx of tourists into the town as summer days became warm enough to enjoy camping, fishing, and hiking near the mountain.

"Nope. Just the usual people. I did see that the grocery store and campground were busy, though. I heard a bunch of people talking about Bigfoot as I left the store on my way here."

"It's about that time again," Reilly said. He had grown up near Tahoma Valley and had worked for the sheriff's office for fifteen years. Almost everyone in the room knew the strange and even sometimes gruesome sights that Reilly had seen.

"Would you turn that crap off?" Troy asked Jessie, who had moved closer to the screen as Zach Larson walked through a dark forest.

She shrugged and changed the channel. "Whatever. I don't usually watch it. George saw that guy at lunch and told me he was the host of that show." She finished her sandwich and left.

Troy placed her dirty plate and glass in a bin behind the counter. "George isn't here tonight."

At the moment, George's brother Carson walked into the bar. He waved to the men and joined the others. "What can I get for you, Carson?" Troy asked.

"I'll have a light beer, bottled," Carson said. Troy named a few brands and Carson made his selection, then turned to the deputies. "Quiet week so far."

"Don't expect that to last," Joey warned. "School's out now and parents are probably anxious to bring their kids up to the scenic points on the mountain, so we'll have our usual flow of traffic through here. Not to mention the Bigfoot nuts."

"Bigfoot nuts?"

Reilly sighed. Joey could sometimes be a bit too blunt. "There are several teams of Bigfoot hunters here. I guess they all belong to some online forum about Bigfoot and there's been a surge in sightings around here the past few weeks."

"So, they all picked this weekend to come up here," Carson sighed. He took a drink from the bottle. "I guess I better make sure I stay on duty at the clinic for most of the weekend."

"This happens most years," Reilly said. "Once they get out here and realize that either someone was making false reports or don't find anything for themselves, they'll leave."

"But they always come back." Joey made a face. "Why June? Isn't Bigfoot supposedly here year-round?" She had often heard the locals talk about the creature, but had never seen one.

"Even Bigfoot likes warmer weather," Troy replied. The others turned to look at him. "What? It's the summer solstice this Saturday night, the weather's getting nice, and there are probably lots of food options out there."

Three men walked into the bar. The people who had been playing pool paused and looked at them. For a moment, the only sound in the room was the game announcer yelling as a player for the home team hit a grand slam.

A short man with dark hair broke the silence. "Hi, I'm Tony Simons. I'm here in town for a few days with my friends Cal and Aaron."

The two other men waved. One was tall and red-haired with a goatee, the other just a bit taller than Tony and also dark-haired with no facial hair. They all wore polo shirts of different colors and jeans.

"We're staying at the campground outside of town," Cal said. "We just dropped by because we had a question about a map."

"What map?" Reilly asked. Joey looked at him, noticing the strain in his voice. Carson, too, suddenly seemed on edge.

"I picked up this brochure a long time ago when I was out

here in high school," Tony replied. He held out a familiar paper booklet. "There seems to be a cave system in the area, but we haven't been able to locate it."

"I don't recall any caves around here," Carson replied. He took another long swig from the bottle. "Are you sure that's for this area?"

Tony turned it around so they could see the words "Tahoma Valley" printed on the front. "I just thought it would be interesting to explore a place I haven't seen around here yet."

"Well, that map must be wrong," Reilly said. He led the group out of the bar and to the rack of brochures in the front lobby. "Here you go." He pulled out the most recent map of Tahoma Valley. "This was printed much more recently than that one." He gently removed the old map from Tony's hands and placed the new one in it. "Enjoy the area, guys."

"But surely those caves were there at one point," Cal persisted.

"Maybe," Reilly agreed. "But who knows what condition they'd be in now? We've had some earthquakes that could have caused some damage. If they are still there, they'd be a poor place to visit."

"Thanks," Tony replied slowly. Joey joined Reilly in the foyer as the three men left the tavern.

"What was that about?" she asked.

Carson came to the door with his car keys out. "You know what it's about, Joey." He looked around to make sure they were alone. "We need to keep people away from the caves."

"We finally made it!" Autumn exclaimed.

Erica pulled out two bags from the trunk. "At least we have everything we need."

Autumn went up to the porch and used her cell phone as light while she unlocked the front door. The events at the ice cream shop and a stop at the grocery store just before it closed had delayed them. Mitzi had been awake when they arrived to check in, though, and had warned them that their neighbor in Cabin 1 would probably already be asleep.

She helped Erica bring the luggage and groceries in, and they placed the cold items in the fridge. Helping herself to a diet pop, Autumn looked out the window and studied the other cabin. It was an A-frame style, with a front porch and a sleeping loft inside. It was closer to the creek than their cabin, but she had noticed that theirs had a fire pit with several chairs and two tables on the side of the building. She hoped their neighbor wouldn't mind their coming and going at odd hours.

"Should we try to let the others know we got to the cabin?" Erica asked. "It's late, but they're probably still up."

"Just text them. I'm tired and ready for bed."

Erica let their friends know they had arrived and invited everyone over for breakfast in the morning. "Good thing we planned on that," she said, studying the contents of the fridge. "Plenty of eggs, and we bought those cinnamon rolls and doughnuts."

"Sounds good." Autumn yawned, finished her drink, and stretched. "Where are the bedrooms?"

"Upstairs. They both have double beds. I'll take the one closest to the stairs and you can have the one overlooking the forest in back. Both rooms have a half-bath, and the main bathroom is down here."

"Okay. I'll shower before everyone gets here tomorrow. See you then." Autumn picked up her bags and went upstairs. The hallway seemed spooky until she turned on a small nightlight on a table between the bedroom doors.

Her bedroom was nicely decorated, with the expected pictures of the mountain and dark green bedding. After using the bathroom and washing her face, she closed the door and changed into pajamas, making sure to pull down the blinds over the windows. She crawled into bed and stared at the ceiling for several minutes. She was hopeful that something big would come of this weekend.

Erica knocked on her door. "Come in," Autumn said,

sitting up and turning on the bedside light.

"I just got a call from Nate. He and Tiffany came by after they got back to the campsite, but we were still at the grocery store. They had an encounter with our neighbor. Guess who he is?"

"Who?" Autumn asked.

"Zach Larson, the host of *Creature Hunt*."

"Oh, dear," Autumn muttered. She smiled. "Now why would he be out here this weekend, when sightings have been at an all-time high in the past few weeks?"

"Nate said Zach told them he was just here on vacation, then went back to his cabin. Maybe we should go over and introduce ourselves tomorrow."

Autumn felt a slight fluttering in her stomach. "Maybe. Or maybe he doesn't want to be disturbed."

"We can at least meet him, either way. There are going to people coming and going from here until Sunday, so it's only nice to explain what we're doing."

"Let's see how we feel in the morning," Autumn said. "Good night, Erica."

"Good night."

Autumn turned off the light and stared at the ceiling again. She'd finally get a chance to meet Zach. She hoped she wouldn't be disappointed if he was completely different from his on-camera personality. Sighing, she closed her eyes. Tomorrow might bring more excitement than she had imagined.

CHAPTER 6

On Friday morning Zach woke up and rolled over. He felt surprisingly refreshed. It had been a long time since he had slept in a bed that was this comfortable. He threw the covers aside and went over to the window, opening the curtain. As was typical in this area, the morning was overcast but he knew the sun would be out when the clouds cleared in a couple of hours.

He showered and walked down the stairs. A coffee pot and packets of coffee were part of the supplies provided by Mitzi, so he started a pot and looked through the fridge for something to eat. He breathed deeply and the smell of coffee overtook his senses. When it was ready, he poured a cup and slipped on his sneakers, then headed outside. There were now two cars parked in front of Cabin 2 and he could hear voices coming from an open window.

From here, he could see a portion of the creek with several boulders on each side, in an almost uniform pattern that Zach rarely saw in nature. Frowning, he walked forward until he was at the edge of the boulders. He looked across the creek at the other bank. He had not previously noticed the large pile of foliage on the other side that seemed to be in the shape of a primitive shelter, but it loomed large in his field of vision now.

Taking a quick look behind him, he noticed that he was just out of sight of the cabin. Any animal that came down here would be hidden until it wanted to be seen. Zach started to feel uneasy, as if he was being watched. He stared across the creek until a knocking sound forced him to look around. Was that a Bigfoot trying to communicate?

The sound came again, and he shook his head. No, someone was at the front door of the cabin. Sound carried well out here. Zach strolled back to the cabin and walked around the side.

An attractive woman stood on the front porch. She was dressed in dark jeans, a t-shirt, and a light fleece jacket. She was slightly overweight, with wavy auburn hair just down to her shoulders. She held a plate in her hands. As Zach watched, she knocked again, then turned around and saw him.

Autumn gasped. She immediately recognized Zach Larson. He was just under six feet tall with a muscular build and green eyes. His blond hair looked damp, as if he was fresh from the shower. He was dressed for the cool morning in jeans, sneakers, and a hooded jacket. His eyes were intense as they focused on her.

"Hi," he said. "Can I help you?"

She smiled. "I'm one of your neighbors here," she said quickly. "My name is Autumn Hunter."

"I'm Zach Larson."

"I know." She blushed. "I mean, I watch your show. It's great. You're great." She mentally cursed herself. "We made some cinnamon rolls and had a few extra, so I thought I'd bring them over."

Zach smiled. The plate smelled wonderful. "Thank you. Both for saying you like the show and the cinnamon rolls." She handed the plate to him.

"We'll be in and out of here for the next couple of days," she said. "We're here to hunt Bigfoot." He saw her blush again.

"Well, good luck with that. I'm here on vacation."

"Oh." She sounded disappointed. "Okay. We may be out late at night, too. We just wanted to warn you in case you heard strange things."

"Thank you," Zach replied. He decided to not remind her that he had heard any number of strange things in the forest before now. It might make her blush again.

"Goodbye," Autumn said quickly, and retreated. She looked back at him when she was halfway to Cabin 2. He waved and went into Cabin 1, closing the door quietly behind him. *Idiot*, she mentally cursed herself. She could have handled that better.

Inside, Zach, set the paper plate on the table and peeled

back the foil. Three cinnamon rolls, with just the right amount of frosting, waited for him. He transferred one of them to a plate from the cupboard and placed it in the microwave for a few seconds. As he sat down to eat his breakfast, he saw that an envelope had been taped to the bottom of the paper plate. Curious, he pulled it out and opened it to find a short note.

"Dear Zach," he read out loud. "If you have a few moments later today I would really like to speak to you for a bit about your views on the Jersey Devil and Bigfoot, and if they could really exist in the same place. Thanks, Autumn."

Despite himself, he smiled. She had seemed nice, and even while on vacation he was already starting to get drawn into the Bigfoot fever that seemed to hang over Tahoma Valley. He took a bite of the cinnamon roll and almost moaned at the delicious flavor. "Yes, Autumn," he replied, speaking in the direction of the window. "You can have a few minutes of my time."

"I'm sure it wasn't that bad," Erica assured Autumn a few minutes later. She had returned to the cabin and immediately started laughing hysterically. Mike, Bill, and Nate had stared at her while Tiffany and Erica had made her sit down at the table to calm down.

"It gets worse. I left a note taped to the plate asking if I could talk to him about the Jersey Devil and Bigfoot. I want to kick myself."

"A skill most people claim they want to have but few actually do want if they think about it," Bill said from the couch. "Relax. I doubt you're the first person who has asked him to talk about what he does for a living. You won't be the last."

"You think so?" Autumn pulled her hands away from her face.

"Yeah," Nate said, putting a hand on her shoulder. He and Autumn had dated for a short time a few years ago before realizing that they were better off being friends.

"Thanks, guys." She smiled. "He did seem nice, at least. Maybe I'll go try speaking to him again later."

"I'll go with you," Nate offered. "Maybe you'll feel more confident about it if a friend is there."

Autumn nodded. "Okay." Tiffany stood, gave Nate a kiss, and hugged him. The two were engaged and planning to get married in the fall.

"Or why not invite him over later for a pre-dinner gathering?" she suggested. "Then we can all meet him. Face it, we're all fans of *Creature Hunt*. I'm sure he's got some interesting stories to tell."

"I'll go over and do that right now," Mike said. "About four o'clock? We can have some drinks and snacks ready."

Autumn nodded. Mike nudged Bill and they walked out the door. Autumn's thoughts returned to the upcoming day. "So, what did you all decide while I was out making a fool of myself?"

"There's a site a few miles down the highway, on the other side of town, where some other people from BOG are set up. They texted me yesterday and claimed to have had an encounter with a large creature last night. I thought we'd head over there and talk to them, see what they've come up with."

"Sounds good," Erica said. "Do you have your laptop, Autumn?"

"Yep. I'll put the rest of my bag together, as well." Autumn stood and stretched. "Let's get ready to catch a Bigfoot."

"That's the spirit," Nate said. He went over to his digital camera. "Yep, it's charged. Tiff, let's check the car to make sure we have what we need."

Tiffany and Nate went outside just as Mike and Bill came back in. "He said he'd be happy to come over," Bill told Autumn and Erica. "On our way back, we'll stop at the store we passed yesterday."

Autumn felt a warm glow spread through her. She was familiar with how her crushes started, and she was hoping to be able to get Zach alone for a few minutes while they were both here at the resort. It wasn't often that she took chances on following her emotions, but this was one time where her instincts were probably going to lead her to a good place. As she went up to her bedroom, she hoped that those same instincts would lead her to finally finding the evidence she was looking for in their search for a monster.

CHAPTER 7

When Autumn and her friends arrived at the designated parking lot, they discovered that several other BOG members from the campground had also come to search in this area. "Looks like we've got a crowd," Bill muttered as he opened the trunk of his car and pulled out his bag.

"There's Tony Simons," Erica pointed out. Everyone on their team scowled. Tony had a fondness for talking down to many of the other BOG members online, and protested every photograph that was posted as being "amateurish and obviously a hoax or a prank." He had once submitted a photo and Nate had been the first to point out that the distant object Tony had identified as Bigfoot was actually clearly Bill, as it had been taken during a weekend gathering like this and the subject of the photo was wearing a dark blue windbreaker. Tony had been quiet online for a few weeks after that, but had recently been more active after a trip down to Arkansas where he had supposedly seen the Boggy Creek monster.

Tony looked their way. Autumn smiled brightly and waved. "Going to get Bill's picture again?" she called out. "I'm sure he'd just send you one if you asked nicely."

Tony gestured with his middle finger and turned back to his companions. "Let's get going," Tiffany said. "According to the site, there are three trails here. One looks like it heads in the direction of Mitzi's Cabin Resort. I've already seen several people head out on the other two trails."

"Sounds good," Mike said. They left the car and headed for the trails. Autumn paused to read the posted guidelines.

"According to this, we shouldn't go off the trail," she said. "How many times have we actually followed these rules?"

"You should definitely stick to the trail," Tony said from behind her, making her jump. She turned and glared at him. "In fact, walk on all of them. You could use the exercise."

"Jackass," Erica muttered from beside Autumn.

Autumn felt her face flush. She stared at Tony, but spoke loudly enough for all his friends to hear. "Kind of smells like you've been hanging out with Bigfoot already, Tony."

His friends laughed. Tony backed away from their group. "Maybe you should keep your investigating to after dark. Keeps the forest prettier."

"Okay, okay," Nate said, pushing his way to the front of the group. "Come on, Autumn. Let's get going." They headed down their designated trail. Bill kept an eye on Tony's group and smiled when he saw them heading in the other direction.

"We might have one or two other teams following us," he stated when they were a quarter of a mile down the path. "I just saw some hints of orange and yellow coats."

"As long as it's not Tony and the slime balls, I don't care," Tiffany said. They hiked another half mile before the group found a spot where they could sit and observe the forest for awhile. Erica set out a blanket and a couple of camping chairs. Autumn unfolded her own chair and found a tree to sit under. She had a glimpse of the sloping hillside from this spot.

Before sitting, she joined Mike and Bill on the path to help them draw a map of their location. "I wonder what's down that direction," she said to Nate, pointing further down the trail. "According to Tiffany, this path should lead us back towards the cabins."

"I'll take a look," he said. "Want to come with me?"

Autumn looked longingly at her chair, but decided this was more important. "Sure. Anyone want to come with us?"

"I will," said Bill.

"I'll wait here," Mike said, sitting in Autumn's chair. He grinned at her. "Just keeping it warm for you, Autumn."

Nate, Autumn, and Bill set out down the path. They could hear other hikers in the area and knew it would be hard to try to attract a Bigfoot with so many other people around. "It's only going to be seen if it wants us to see it," Bill pointed out. "That's the downside of coming to places like this when frequent sightings are reported."

Autumn suddenly stopped and Nate almost walked into

her. "What?" he said quietly, seeing her become tense.

"What's that?" she whispered. She pointed at a large indentation at the very edge of the trail.

Nate got out his camera and kneeled down. "Maybe the heel end of a footprint?"

Bill examined it, as well. "Maybe."

Autumn gingerly put her own foot down to the side of the impression. "Where was it going?" she asked, feeling her leg drop down. "It's a pretty steep drop."

She knew she should have heeded her own warning when she suddenly slipped on some leaves. She felt her body hit the side of the hill. As Autumn slid several feet down through the brush, she winced at the pain from dead branches hitting her arms. Thankfully, the extremely large root of a tree stopped her from tumbling down the rest of the hillside.

"Oh shit, are you okay?" she heard Nate ask from the top of the hill. "Autumn?"

"Yeah, I'm here," she managed to say. She saw Bill looking over the edge. "I think I just maybe need a hand to help me up."

Both men kneeled and reached down to her. She found her footing on a couple of logs and jumped enough to grab their hands. They pulled her back onto the trail. Four other people had joined them by now. "That was embarrassing," she said, feeling her face flush again.

"I don't think that's a Bigfoot print," someone from the other group said, looking at it. "There's some tread at the bottom."

Bill looked at it again. "Damn. So, who walked off the cliff?"

"Maybe someone's playing a joke on us," someone else in the group replied. "We went down the rest of this trail as far as we could. There's a pile of logs across the path and signs saying 'End of path' so we came back this way."

Autumn, Nate, and Bill followed the others back to their own team. "What happened?" Erica cried when she saw Autumn's dirty jeans and sweatshirt. Mike stood up from the chair, where he had been typing something on his phone.

"Oh, I took a slight fall. I'll be fine."

"Are you sure?"

"Yep." Autumn said down in her chair. She brushed off her jeans and winced. She'd need to check when they got back to the cabin to make sure nothing was really injured, but she was pretty sure she'd only have a couple of bruises and some scratches. She got out her computer and opened it up. "Anything happening here yet?"

"Nope." The group settled down and fell quiet. The sounds of other teams seemed to be getting more distant. At one point, silence finally seemed to reign through the forest.

"Now?" Mike whispered. Everyone nodded. He located a long piece of wood, went over to the tree next to Autumn, and whacked the branch against the tree three times. They always tried to make sure they were alone in area when attempting to locate a Bigfoot with wood knocks. Otherwise, other groups might answer them the same way and cause confusion for everyone.

Autumn noted the time in her open file and her notebook. The group waited for five minutes, eyes either on the forest in front of them or the trail leading to the highway behind them. "Second try," Mike whispered, and knocked three more times.

This time, they received a response. Three solid knocks came from Autumn's left, down the trail that they had explored earlier. She noted the approximate location.

"We were just down there," Bill said in amazement. Nate picked up another branch and walked to the other side of the path. He knocked twice.

When another response came, this time with two knocks, Autumn started to get excited. "Something's out there," she whispered.

Mike gave three knocks on his tree, but the group waited five minutes and no response came. Nate tried again on his tree. No response. Erica checked the recorder. "I didn't get much directly, but we can review these later."

"I think we should do this again tonight," Tiffany said. Autumn was surprised to hear her say that. While Tiffany was a member of their team, she often left the active investigating to Nate. Maybe the responses to the knocks were encouraging to her.

"Not at the campground," Bill said. "Too many people around, and I think we should try the call blasts."

"How about at the resort?" Autumn asked. "I can ask Mitzi for permission and let her know that we'll be playing some howls and whoops."

"I think quiet time is at eleven," Erica pointed out. "We'd have to be done by then."

"Let's go out around nine or so. There will still be a little light, at least for the beginning. We're far enough away from every cabin except Zach's that the other guests shouldn't get too disturbed, and we can let him know what we're doing. Heck, maybe he'll want to come along."

They all agreed to a night investigation. "Meanwhile," Mike said, looking at his watch, "I think it's time for lunch."

They decided to meet back at the campground. On their way out, they noticed Tony and his friends just emerging from their area of the forest. "Did you hear the wood knocks?" Tony asked Nate. "I think something out there was playing with us."

"Some of those were ours," Nate replied. "And then we got responses."

Tony looked disappointed. "Where were the responses coming from?"

Autumn looked around Nate. "I think down from your direction. Maybe you were closer than you think."

He nodded. "I figured that. We found some footprints that looked like they were going off the trail. We'll be back to cast them this afternoon."

"Good luck," Erica said. She gestured to the car and Autumn got in. She wished Tony wasn't here, but didn't want to let his presence ruin what could otherwise be a good investigation. She had misled him about the knocks on purpose. The responses had come from somewhere down closer to the cabins, where the trail had supposedly been blocked off from travel. Something was going on down there, and she was determined to give her group a chance to find that evidence before any other team.

CHAPTER 8

After seeing the BOG members leave, Zach immediately put on his boots, glad that he had decided to bring them. Making sure his camera, measuring equipment, and notepad were in his backpack, he added a sweatshirt and a granola bar. He left his cabin and set out in the sunshine to walk to the edge of the creek.

The water was shallow and Zach was able to walk across on several large stones with no problems. The tree pile loomed over him as he approached it. There was a defined entrance to the shelter. The entrance faced the forest, and Zach walked away from it to the tree line. Although he was just under six feet tall, he felt sure that even something a couple of feet taller would be able to move freely between this shelter and the safety of the tree cover without being noticed. He sat on a tree stump for a moment and quietly observed his surroundings.

This was the perfect environment for a Bigfoot. The creek would provide water and maybe the occasional fish or small reptile. There was constant shade during the day. During the winter, if snow reached this level, a path could be made for easy access to hunting and foraging. He sketched the area, making note of the squirrels running around and even the deer that he could see between the trees in the distance.

He looked around nervously. There were really only two options for the existence of this structure. Either a human had built it as a quiet place for sleeping and seeking away from most of the elements, or a Bigfoot had built it for the same reasons. The structure was nearly ten feet high at the tallest point of the branches, and he brought out his measuring tape and noted as he walked from one edge to the other that it was about twelve feet long. Surely he was not the first person to notice this, as it was easily visible just steps away from his cabin.

Zach placed his backpack on the ground and took several pictures of the structure with his camera. He wrote down the measurements and noted down his growing feeling that he was being watched. He looked up from the notepad and realized that he could see Mitzi crossing the field between his cabin and Cabin 2. He made a note to interview her later, and placed the pen and paper back in his bag.

He stood at the doorway of the structure and turned on his flashlight. As expected, there was nothing inside. There was an intensely bad odor, though, and any thoughts Zach may had still have about humans building this structure were starting to fade. Excitement began to rise up in him, replacing the nervousness. While this didn't exactly fall under the solid proof side of evidence, he could at least show that some animal had built itself a home. And was smart enough to do so with the doorway facing the forest rather than a place where people would see it coming in and going out.

He backed away and looked across the creek again. Mitzi had moved on to the next group of cabins. Zach decided to walk down one of the paths that were laid out at the entrance to the tree line. Figuring that he might find more evidence down the path that was directly across from the shelter, he put on his sweatshirt and set out with his bag firmly on his back, camera in his front pocket, and flashlight in hand. It crossed his mind that the flashlight was the only tool he had on him that could be used as a weapon.

After almost two miles, he had not seen anything out of place and was getting hungry. He found another large stump and settled down. The simple granola bar he had packed an hour ago now seemed like the best-tasting bit of food he had had all day, and was enjoying it when he heard three loud knocks in the distance.

Zach stopped eating and stayed silent, his hand next to his flashlight. The sound had come from somewhere in front of him, down the path he had already walked on. He waited, and two more knocks sounded through the trees. This time, they appeared to be ahead of him, and very close.

Zach felt his muscles tighten and the hairs on his neck began to stand up. He was about to grab the flashlight and run back to the creek when he heard a shout come from somewhere down the path. In the distance, he saw several people gathered in a group on one side of the trail. He realized that the path must be a way to get out here from the main part of town and was probably fairly well-traveled.

He no longer felt like he was being watched. He decided to go back to the creek, carefully walk past the shelter, and return to the resort so he could talk to Mitzi. She must have seen something; after all, she had been running the camping cabins for nearly twenty years.

He thought he recognized a couple of the people on the trail. Autumn's jacket stood out from the green branches. Her friend Bill, who had come over to invite Zach to have a snack with them this afternoon, was rather tall and he thought he recognized him as well. Zach smiled. He'd ask them what they were doing out here when he saw them later.

When Zach reached the structure again, he paused. There were two large footprints near the shelter, leading towards the door. He knew for a fact that they had not been there when he had arrived. He paused, wondering if he should look inside the shelter again.

A rustling of leaves at his back made up his mind. He ran across the creek and to his cabin, not pausing to look back. Despite having spent many long nights looking for monsters such as Bigfoot, he was not anxious to come face to face with one by himself without any protection.

He sat down on the couch and reviewed the pictures from his camera. They were all good shots. He placed his camera on the side table and walked over to the convenience store.

Luckily, Mitzi was in the store having a conversation with the clerk. "Hello, Mr. Larson," she greeted him. "Anything you need today?"

"A few moments of your time, if you can spare them."

Mitzi smiled. "Of course. Come on over to the booths back here. Would you like something to drink?"

"Diet pop, please."

Mitzi got the beverages and settled down across from

Zach. "I'll be honest, Mr. Larson…"

"Please call me Zach."

"Okay, Zach. I think I know why you want to talk to me and I'm trying to decide if I should send you to someone who's seen what you're after."

Zach leaned forward, trying to keep his voice down as three other guests entered the store. "Technically, I'm on vacation. But the people staying across from me are looking for Bigfoot, and I guess you could say that as of this morning I'm an interested party as well."

"The tree shelter across the creek?" Mitzi asked, also keeping her voice low while waving and nodding at the other customers.

"Yes. I saw it this morning. Does something actually live there?"

"I think so. It's not the first one that's been built. Some of the men in town took down the others. I try to fill those two cabins last because I'm honestly not sure how a guest would react if they saw a large hairy beast staring at them from such a short distance away."

Zach nodded. "I think I almost had a close encounter with one this morning. Who's this person you think I should talk to?"

"He's an older gentleman, living just a couple of miles away. He's seen a lot and tells quite a few stories. I think some of them might be true."

"About Bigfoot?"

Mitzi looked around to see if anyone else was listening. "Yes."

"If I go see him, I'll want to take along at least one member of the BOG group. Do you think he'd be okay with that?"

Mitzi winked. "Why don't you bring along that pretty woman Autumn? She seemed smart, with a good head on her shoulders."

"Maybe I'll ask her about that. What's this guy's name?"

"Stanley Smith. He's got a couple of sons down here in

Tahoma Valley. George and Carson."

"I think I've already encountered George," Zach said. Mitzi wrote down an address for him.

"I'll give him a call to warm him up a bit and let him know I gave you his information. When would you want to drop by?"

"Tomorrow afternoon," Zach replied. "I need some time to think about what I saw and experience the town tonight."

"Let me guess. You're going to the Valley Tavern."

"Seems like it might be a hopping place on a Friday night," Zach replied with his own wink. "Maybe I'll see George there again."

"George and all his friends. The deputies like to come by as well just to keep an eye on things. We look out for each other around here."

"I can see that," Zach said. "Thanks, Mitzi." He took his bottle of soda with him and walked back to his cabin. Autumn and Erica had not yet returned. He hoped they were having some success in their search.

CHAPTER 9

Zach knocked on the door of Cabin 2. He had seen the BOG crew arrive about an hour earlier, speaking excitedly to each other. He wondered if he should tell them about his exploration across the creek earlier today. Keeping silent might mean possible danger if they decided to go over there, but from what he had seen so far, the group's attention was focused on other parts of Tahoma Valley. As he heard someone coming down the stairs inside, he decided that he would stay silent on the topic unless it was necessary to warn them about the structure.

Autumn opened the door. She had changed her clothes after her arrival an hour ago. When she had walked into the house, she had been dusty and looked tired. Now, she was clean and smelled faintly of vanilla. She smiled at him. "Hi, Zach. The others are getting some snacks ready. We thought we'd sit out at the picnic tables. It's such a nice day."

"Sure," Zach agreed. He stepped back to let her pass, and she closed the door behind her. They walked around the side of the house to where Tiffany and Nate were setting out beverages on one of the tables. Nate shook Zach's hand and introduced himself, then invited Zach to sit down. Tiffany introduced herself and gave him the beer he requested from the table.

"What made you decide to come to Mount Rainier this weekend?" Nate asked. "I mean, I know we're here because of so much activity on the BOG message board. Autumn said you were here on vacation."

"That's right," Zach said. "I called one of my cameramen before I came up and he warned me that there had been Bigfoot sightings in the area. I wanted a few days away from my usual routine, though, so I decided to come up here anyway."

"What's been your favorite investigation so far?" Tiffany asked as Erica, Mike, and Bill stepped outside with trays of food and joined them. "The show has been on for two seasons. Are there really that many more cryptids out there to investigate?"

"You'd be surprised at the e-mails and phone calls that come in about local monsters and legends," Zach replied. Autumn got up to serve herself, and he followed her. "We did go back to the site of two previous investigations, once in upstate New York and once in Wisconsin."

He took some cheese, crackers, and deli meat from the platters. "I made the cookies," Autumn murmured to him. He smiled and looked down at the selection.

"Chocolate chip, my favorite," he whispered back. They settled down again next to the fire pit. Bill struggled to get some logs and kindling arranged in the perfect way, and finally a flame burst forth from under the pile.

"Also, you may have noticed that we've done some episodes on things that weren't really what people would usually consider to be the classic 'lurking in the woods' type of monster. We interviewed some people who claimed to be vampires, as well as looked for giant rodents. I think that's one reason the producer gave us a break right about now. They need to sort through all the requests that people have sent in to decide where to take the show during the third season."

"New episodes are on right now, aren't they?" Tiffany asked. "Wasn't there one last night?"

"You mean you missed that one?" Zach said, but he smiled and winked.

"I saw some of it online," Nate confessed. "I believe you were investigating the Jersey Devil."

"Yep, that was a good one. It seemed like more people were open about their sightings than most other cryptids we investigate. And we did have a scary moment where one of the cameramen actually felt something grab onto his shoulders." Zach paused, thinking about that night. Brandon had been terrified to feel claws digging into his skin. Once whatever had grabbed on to him had let go, he had run for the van and refused to come out. When he finally took off his shirt at the hotel that night, he had scratches on his shoulder despite wearing three layers of clothing. The other crew members had been uneasy about going back into the forest the next evening.

Zach shook his head, bringing himself back to the present. "As for my favorite, I think that's when we were in upstate New York doing the episode about the lake monster, nicknamed Champ, in Lake Champlain. The area was beautiful, we had a lot of great witnesses to talk to, and the people we hired to take us out on the lake were very professional."

"You still didn't find anything," Bill pointed out.

"Nope, but that's the way it is most of the time. I suppose most of these creatures don't want to be found."

"I left a note for you this morning," Autumn interjected. "It seems kind of silly now, but do you think that Bigfoot and the Jersey Devil could be in the same place?"

"That calls for some wild speculation," Zach answered.

"That's pretty much what we do on the forum," Nate said. "Speculate away."

Zach gathered his thoughts as he took another sip of beer. "I think Bigfoot and the Jersey Devil could probably co-exist if the situation was right. They'd have to eat to survive. If there was an area that could provide sources of food and water, I don't see why both creatures couldn't be in one place."

"Can you imagine what that would be like?" Autumn asked in awe. "To go in search of one cryptid and find others in the same place?"

"Are there really such creatures as werewolves?" Erica asked. "I know about all the dog-man sightings out in the Midwest, but as far as I know no one has ever actually seen one transform from human into beast."

Zach took a sip of beer before replying. "First thing I have to admit, I'm still a skeptic at heart about most of the creatures we go out to search for. I want evidence, something that I can hold in my hand or have scientists examine in a lab.

I still have some trouble believing in such things as ghosts or the traditional idea of a werewolf. I can believe that there might be creatures out there looking like wolves that can walk upright and interact with humans."

Autumn nodded. "Have you had any close encounters? Not with aliens. I mean times when you thought that maybe there actually was something with you."

"We did have something bump our boat hard enough to throw me and several other people off-balance when we were on Lake Champlain," Zach admitted. "Whatever it was managed to stay just out of reach of our camera. And there was the time in West Virginia when we were chasing down a supposed goat-like monster when I started to feel a pull towards a dangerous hillside. I truly believe I could see something beckoning for me to come to it, a large figure with horns on its head. Luckily, one of the cameramen saw me walking and pulled me back from the edge of a cliff just in time."

"Wow," everyone breathed at once. Zach ate in silence for a bit as the others talked, then he relaxed again and breathed in the scent of the campfire.

"So where were you all today?" he asked casually during a break in the conversation. "I saw Autumn and Erica heading out late morning."

"We met up with some other people on the BOG forum," Bill said. "They're a few miles away, and they said they saw a Bigfoot along the lake last week. They've been out here since then trying to get another glimpse."

"Any pictures?"

"A blurry one," Mike admitted. "The usual kind of thing that gets people like us mocked in public and online."

"We did find some footprints, and Autumn fell off the trail," Nate added.

"Did you get hurt?" Zach asked her.

"No. We didn't see much else."

"That happens way too often," Erica said bitterly. She added another small piece of wood to the fire. "At least this weekend we can meet with like-minded people."

Zach watched Autumn. She looked back at him and smiled. He suddenly felt happy and wondered what her life was like beyond the monster hunting. He also wondered if she'd give him a chance to get to know her better.

The group chatted for several more minutes. Nate finally looked at his watch. "Oh, wow. We need to get back to the campsite and get dinner started."

"Would you like to join me and Erica for dinner?" Autumn asked shyly. "We're just making something light here. We'll be up late tonight and want to take a short nap." She suddenly blushed. Had she actually just suggested that Zach take a nap with her?

Zach smiled. "Thank you for the offer, but I have other plans for the evening. Hopefully I can see you again later." That his plans included dinner by himself at the tavern and watching television all night was his own secret. His interest in this group of friends was still in the beginning stages, and he didn't want to impose on what was obviously a single-minded mission for the weekend.

"Okay," she said, a little disappointed. What was going on with her? She couldn't decide if she wanted to go over to Zach and kiss him or ignore him and hope that he didn't think she and her friends were fools.

"Are you going to be around later?" Mike asked, saving Autumn from her feelings. "We'll be out in the woods near here later tonight doing an investigation. You're welcome to come with us."

"Thanks, but I'll pass this time. I'd be interested in hearing about anything you might find, though."

"Great."

Zach stood and Autumn walked with him around the side of the cabin. "We enjoyed chatting with you," she said. "I hope I'll see you again before the weekend is over."

"I'm quite certain you will," he said, and smiled. He walked back over to his cabin. He'd relax for awhile and then head over to the tavern. With all the other action going on in town, he thought it could be an interesting evening.

CHAPTER 10

Zach managed to find a parking spot in the lot outside the Valley Tavern. He pulled in next to an old truck that had two coolers in the back. The strong smell of fish and some dried blood told Zach that the coolers probably held the results of a day spent near a lake and in the forest. The truck was at the very end of the parking lot, and Zach noticed that there wasn't a light pole overhead. Indeed, this corner of the lot was rather dark although several spots nearby were illuminated.

When he opened the door, he was not surprised to see that the dining room was full and there were several people waiting on the vinyl benches lining the entryway. He went into the bar and noticed that although it was busy, it actually seemed less chaotic than the dining room. He took a seat near the end of the bar, on the far side so he could face the doorway and see if anyone interesting came in to the tavern.

He nodded at a group around one of the pool tables. Several of them were the same men who had been here yesterday at lunch time, but there were also new faces. A group of young women took up another game table. Zach, uninterested in pool, looked down at the drink menu that one of the bartenders had placed in front of him.

"New here in town?" the guy asked.

"Just vacationing for the weekend. Is it always this busy here?"

"Friday's usually busy, but this is a big crowd even for a weekend," the bartender said. "You waiting for a table?"

"Can I eat here?"

"Sure. I'll bring back a food menu for you. My name's Troy, by the way."

"I'm Zach. For now, I'll just have a beer. Bottled, not draft." He pointed to the brand.

Troy nodded and served him, then briefly disappeared. The other bartender appeared to be older than Troy and was having an extended conversation with a couple of men on the other side. When Zach had walked past them, he had overheard something about the sheriff's office, so he assumed they were connected to law enforcement.

He saw George emerge from the crowd in the hallway and enter the bar. George joined his friends at a pool table, picking up a glass that was already half-empty and drinking from it. Zach surmised that he had been in the bathroom or gone into the dining room for some reason. One of the other men said something to George and nodded in Zach's direction. George turned and gave a small smile.

"Here you go," Troy said, placing the familiar menu in front of Zach.

"I tried the club sandwich yesterday. What do you recommend for dinner?"

"The meatloaf is good. So is the spaghetti. Comes with a great meat sauce."

"I just need a couple of minutes."

Troy nodded and turned to someone else. Zach was looking through his choices when someone sat down next to him. He looked up and saw that one of the law enforcement men had joined him. "Hi," the other guy said. "I'm Reilly Brown, a sheriff's deputy for the county."

"Nice to meet you, Deputy Brown. I'm Zach Larson."

"I recognized you from your show."

Zach sighed. "I've been getting that a lot this weekend. I thought I could escape it by coming here."

"Not with that Bigfoot-hunting group here in town. I'm surprised they're not lined up at the door trying to talk to you."

Zach smiled. "A few of them are staying at the cabin next to me down at Mitzi's. They're a nice group. Dedicated to their beliefs, I'll say that."

Reilly snorted as a tall woman came up to him. "Dedicated to craziness." He turned to the woman, a stocky brunette with short hair. "Joey Singleton, this is Zach Larson. He's the host of a show called *Creature Hunt*."

Joey nodded at him. "Nice to meet you. Reilly, can we

speak for a few minutes?"

"Sure. Aren't you on patrol tonight?"

"Yep. That's why I need to talk to you."

"Excuse me," Reilly said to Zach. He headed for the doorway with the other deputy, both of their postures tense as they left the building.

Zach signaled to Troy. "I'll have an order of mozzarella sticks to start, and then I'll get the bacon cheeseburger."

Troy smiled. "Nice choice." He added a glass of water to the counter in front of Zach and picked up a phone, apparently to call the order over to the kitchen. Zach turned around on his stool. The man who had been sitting with Reilly looked at his phone and also left the bar. George and his fellow pool players looked relaxed and seemed to be enjoying themselves. Zach smiled and watched the rest of the people around him for several minutes until Troy returned with his appetizer.

"Here you go. The cheeseburger probably won't be too far behind. Forgot to ask, did you want a salad or fries with that?"

Zach bit into a mozzarella stick and smiled. "Fries," he announced. Zach finished the appetizer and finally pulled out his cell phone. He wasn't expecting much, and indeed the only message he had received so far was a text message from one of the producers asking when he'd be available to start filming again. Zach considered his calendar, enjoying how empty it was. He gave the producers a date several weeks away and then put the phone back in his jacket pocket.

When his cheeseburger arrived, he had time to take a couple of bites before the tavern door opened and Reilly and Joey came back inside. They headed straight for George and said something to him. Zach saw George's face go pale and one of his buddies said something back to the deputies. Joey nodded. They all headed outside. Heads turned throughout the bar and the entryway to follow their progress. Curious, Zach took a couple of fries from the plate, dipped them in barbecue sauce, and put them in his mouth before standing up and following the group out to the parking lot.

He wasn't alone. Several of the pool players followed him. Zach caught up to Reilly and Joey as they stopped beside his car and pointed at the truck beyond it. George kicked one of the tires. "God damn it, not again!" he shouted. "This is the second fucking time this week!"

Zach approached and looked around the group. The back of George's truck had been punched in a couple of places, and the tailgate was askew. The two coolers in the back had been thrown on the ground and emptied. Three fish were still on the ground, laid out in a trail leading beyond the logs surrounding the parking lot. Blood from the second cooler formed a parallel track. One of the cooler lids had been thrown against a tree and shattered.

"Calm down, George," Joey ordered. To Zach's surprise, George seemed to relax. "At least this time it wasn't at your house."

"They've been following me," George hissed at the deputies. Seeing Zach, he suddenly stood up straight and shut his mouth.

"Excuse me, Mr. Larson. This is a crime scene," Joey said as Zach took some pictures with his cell phone. He noticed that he was not the only one who had pulled out his phone. Several of the men with George appeared to be making calls or sending text messages.

"Vandalism?" Zach asked. "Seems like someone wanted dinner."

"There are often hermits living out in the forest who seek out easy food," Reilly said. "George has left the results of his hunting in the back of his truck many times."

"Yeah," George said. He seemed to take some comfort from Reilly's statement. "Must be one of those crazy people down on the ridge."

Zach had his doubts. He decided it was time to back off, though. He wanted to get back to his dinner.

"Okay," he said with a smile. He walked past everyone

who had gathered outside. It looked like it would be some time before he could get back to his car, anyway. He might as well enjoy the food and atmosphere of the Valley Tavern while he was waiting.

When he arrived back at the bar, it was still busy. Troy had turned on the baseball game. Zach watched it as he finished one of the best burgers he had ever eaten.

He was looking over a dessert menu Troy had provided when he saw Reilly and Joey come back in. George had disappeared, along with most of his friends. Several young women came into the bar behind the deputies and shouts of recognition went up. For a moment Joey looked confused, then with a glance behind her nodded at several of the women. Reilly spoke to a couple of men, and came back over to sit on the stool next to Zach.

"Busy night?" Zach asked. Troy came over and raised his eyebrows. "I'll have the chocolate cake."

"Best in town," Reilly said. "My sister owns the bakery down the road that provides the desserts here."

"I'll second that," Troy said, and after collecting a couple of other orders he once again placed a call to the kitchen.

"What's the story with George and his truck?" Zach asked. "I heard him say that it had been attacked before."

"We've got vandals out here just like any other area," Reilly answered. "Some people come in from out of town and think that Tahoma Valley is the perfect place to drop their inhibitions. A lot of the locals are dedicated to stopping that way of thinking."

"Yeah, but why would someone take some fish? I don't buy that some hermit just wandered by and decided to check the coolers. Was there anything else in them?"

"I think you better let us ask the questions around here," Reilly said, and placed his hat on his head. "Duty calls. Good night, Mr. Larson."

He and Joey left, and the cake arrived. Zach enjoyed it, but many questions went through his mind as the crowd around him continued to grow. Finally, he paid his bill and went out the door. When he reached his car, he found an envelope placed on the windshield.

As he got into the car, he looked around. Nobody was near him, and George had driven away. A dead fish was the only sign that anything odd had taken place here tonight. Zach shrugged, locked his doors, and opened the envelope.

Two brochures slid out. He had seen similar ones in the office and general store at the resort. Zach held them up side by side and discovered that they were nearly identical. "Look here first," had been written on the one in his left hand. He did so, taking time to notice that the spots featured were good areas for hikers and nature explorers. A series of caves roughly five miles from the resort took up a full-page display. Zach looked at the date on the back of the brochure and noticed that it had been printed eleven years ago.

He then turned his attention to the other brochure. The cover and most of the inside attractions were identical, with some updates. He looked through the whole thing, then frowned and looked through again. The caves had been left out of the more recent brochure. He looked at the date and noticed that it had been printed nine years ago.

So, sometime between eleven and nine years ago, someone responsible for tourism in Tahoma Valley had decided that the caves were no longer worth mentioning to visitors. Zach wondered why, and he knew that he needed to find the caves and wondered if the BOG members already knew about them. They might turn out to be an interesting place to look for Bigfoot.

He found a phone number handwritten on the second brochure with a message. "Please call me tomorrow. There's something you need to know about Tahoma Valley. George Smith." He frowned.

Zach had been in a lot of creepy situations. The atmosphere in this town was starting to make him feel on edge. He checked his rearview mirror and thought he could see a shadowy figure next to a tree just outside the parking lot. He looked away, then checked again. The shadowy figure was gone. He sped out of the parking lot, ready to be back at his cabin for the night.

Tony Simons and his friends Aaron and Cal had followed the group out to the parking lot. When everyone else had gone back in, they looked at the dead fish that were still remaining in the parking lot. "He took the fish," Tony said excitedly. "Come on, Bigfoot can't be too far away."

Cal looked skeptical. "If I were him and heard all the noise that was out here just now, I'd be as far away as possible."

"We need to follow him," Tony insisted.

"Come on, Tony. We were out in the woods all day. Let's go back in and enjoy our dinner."

"You're bailing out on me, huh? Thought we were going to stick together this weekend."

Aaron sighed. "Tony, is this because you ran into Autumn and Nate and their friends earlier? I don't know what upsets you about them."

"This isn't a competition," Cal said, drawing a glare from both of his friends. "I mean, we all benefit no matter who finds proof of Bigfoot. So what if it's us or someone else?"

"I want to be the first," Tony demanded. He felt rage rise inside of him at the thought of any other team from the BOG forum beating him to finally decisively proving the existence of Bigfoot. He wanted to show Autumn Hunter and her friends that he was more important than them when it came to cryptid discovery.

"Come on, Tony," Aaron said. "Cal's right, at least for tonight. We're tired, and we have all day tomorrow."

"Except it's night and we know he's been here recently. Screw you guys. I'm going by myself." Tony, filled with anger and trying to hide the fact that he was actually uneasy about being alone in the woods by himself, marched to his car and retrieved his flashlight and a digital camera.

Cal and Aaron watched him. They were both used to his tantrums by now. Tony was dedicated to being the first to find Bigfoot and drag the creature into the public realm. He wanted the glory that would come with the discovery. He worked in the biology department at a local university as a lab technician and they knew that he thought making this discovery would elevate him to a level he couldn't currently reach on his own.

"Fifteen minutes," Cal said. Tony turned and shined the flashlight at the ground near Cal's feet. "Fifteen minutes. If you're not back by then, we'll come looking for you and drag you back here. If Bigfoot is nearby like you think he is, that shouldn't be a problem."

"Fine," Tony snapped. He ran a hand through his hair. "Go back inside, cowards."

He stomped off. Aaron and Cal stayed in the lot long enough to watch him disappear into the misty trees. "Cowards?" Aaron said. "I think we're the smart ones to stay behind this time."

"I think so, too," Cal replied. "Let's keep an eye on the time, though. Come on, our food is probably cold by now." They went back inside the tavern.

Once Tony was beyond the edge of the parking lot and behind some bushes, he stopped to take a couple of deep breaths. He had never told the other members of his team that he had always been terrified of the forest at night. During the day, he was able to lead the team into any terrain where he thought they might find something left behind by Bigfoot. Whether it was hair, prints, feces, or any other sign that the creature could be in the area, he was willing to go to almost any lengths to get it. Only Aaron had ever questioned why the team didn't go on any night hunts, and Tony had always been able to say something that satisfied most of the other team members.

Still, he knew that Cal and Aaron had been walking around the campsite last night with a tape recorder, hoping for some calls from the darkness. Tony had stayed safely in the RV, tucked away in his bedroom at the back, trying to fall asleep. A couple of times he had thought he heard something brush against the camper, and insisted to himself that it was probably a deer or a raccoon. He had only been able to really relax when Aaron and Cal had returned and locked the door behind them.

He looked around him, grateful for the flashlight. He could not go back into the tavern and face Aaron and Cal until at least fifteen minutes had gone by. He saw a silvery flash of fish scales in the light and nodded. At least he could keep himself occupied.

Trying to ignore hoots and distant noises from other animals, he walked through the foliage and was surprised to see part of a fish body on what appeared to be a well-worn trail. Tony kept his concentration on what was ahead of him. More fish pieces appeared as he walked, until suddenly half of a trout had been dropped at the edge of a clearing. He swung his flashlight across the clearing and saw nothing else.

Shrugging, Tony got out his camera and took some pictures, cursing at the darkness. He wanted to gather every bit of evidence he could get. No human he knew would tear off pieces of fish as they walked down a trail and drop them, and then suddenly drop the rest of the fish.

"Why would Bigfoot do that?" he wondered out loud. He checked his watch. It was almost time to head back.

He suddenly realized that everything around him had fallen silent. The hair on the back of his neck tingled, and he realized that something was watching him. "Oh no," he breathed, and his terror came back. This was what he feared. The dark trees and the bushes suddenly seemed to be reaching out for him, trying to keep him here in the woods.

He turned around to follow the path and couldn't find the fish. Something had been behind him, picking up the pieces. His flashlight hit some fish scales, and he headed in that direction. He picked his way through the bushes, aware that the lights in the distance belonged to the tavern.

A loud crack behind him made Tony turn around. He screamed, a sound he never thought he'd hear from his own body. His eyes felt like they would jump out of his head, and his legs suddenly went weak.

A large ape-like creature stood in front of him. It was dark-haired, with a face that stared stonily at Tony. Unlike what he had always heard, the arms didn't hang down past its knees but seemed in proportion with its body. Its eyes made Tony think that he was simply looking at an unusually large and hairy man.

Shaking, he managed to bring his camera up to his face. Bigfoot watched him. As he aimed the device at the creature, Bigfoot swung its hand and hit Tony's arm. Tony screamed in pain, seeing that his wrist had been broken and was now almost horizontal to his arm.

The creature howled, and Tony tried to back away. His injured arm hit a tree. "Damn!" he swore. He turned to look at Bigfoot, and it raised its hand again. Tony felt a sharp pain in his head before everything turned dark and silent.

CHAPTER 11

Autumn greeted Mike and Bill when she arrived at the campground to pick them up for the investigation. "Are you ready?" she asked excitedly. "Erica and Tiffany found a quiet spot close to the cabins where we can set up for the night."

"Good," Bill replied. "Let's get the equipment ready."

Autumn helped them gather voice recorders, video recorders, and digital cameras. They made sure to bring pens and paper to make notes, and lanterns and flashlights. Bill grabbed some canvas camping chairs and Mike grabbed their bag of snacks. Mitzi had told them they could be out until almost midnight as they long as they did the call blasting before eleven. At least a couple of people in the group normally got hungry while sitting outside during the night.

Mike and Bill started discussing what their neighbors at the campsite had said to them while Autumn drove back to the cabin. She pulled in and noticed that Zach's curtains were closed. The lights were on and she could barely make out an outline of his body as he sat on the couch watching television. She hoped he'd reconsider their offer to join in on the investigation. He seemed like someone who could be relied upon to gather facts and sort information.

Erica waved as they entered the cabin. Tiffany and Nate were getting their own equipment set up. "We're going to go about a quarter of a mile west of the cabin," Erica said. "When I went out there a couple of hours ago it was far enough that I couldn't see lights from any of the cabins and couldn't hear much, either."

"We can play the calls?" Bill asked. "Will that concern the neighbors?"

"We let Mitzi know what was going on. If you want to do any calls, let's do them right after we get set up so it's not too late."

Autumn looked at the clock. "It's half past nine. We should probably head out there."

The BOG members gathered all of their investigation

equipment and walked into the forest. Autumn lingered to make sure the cabin was locked and the porch light was on. She looked nervously over at Cabin 1 and bit her lip. She sent a text to Erica stating that she'd be a few minutes behind them and walked to Zach's front door. Before she could knock, the door opened and he smiled at her.

"Hi, Autumn. Would you like to come in?"

"No, thanks. I just wanted to remind you that we're going to be out in the forest late tonight. We have our equipment ready and we're going to try to see if we can draw a Bigfoot to us."

Zach sat down on one of the porch chairs and gestured for her to join him. "Really? How do you plan to do that?"

"We're going to set up and play some animal calls, then Bill will do his own version of a Bigfoot howl. We're also going to try knocking on trees. You've done those before on your show."

"The wood knocks, sure. The calls I used were taken from what was recorded during someone else's investigation."

Autumn decided to be direct. "Zach, do you believe that Bigfoot exists?"

Zach sighed. He thought for a couple of minutes, and Autumn remained quiet. Finally, he smiled weakly. "I'd like to know for sure that it exists."

"What evidence would convince you?"

"The same kind that would convince most people, I think. Dead bodies that we could examine inside and out, clear photos, hair and skin samples that can't be explained away as any other animal or animal hybrid."

"What creature do you most want to find?"

Before Zach could answer, a chilling howl emanated from the forest. Autumn's back stiffened and she felt chilled. Zach stood up and stared off into the distance. He had heard that sound before. He turned to Autumn. "Was that from your group?"

"I don't think so," she whispered. "That didn't sound like any of the calls we use."

Another howl came, followed by a deeper call in response. "Oh shit, there's two of them," Zach said. "Let's go inside."

"No. I want to join my friends."

To her surprise, Zach nodded. "Then let me walk you out there," he said quietly. He retrieved his backpack and a flashlight from the cabin and closed the doors, leaving on the lights.

Autumn jumped off the front porch and began to stride into the forest. She felt Zach's hand on her shoulder. "Hold on. You're just going to go running into an area where we heard howls from two animals? Let's walk slowly and be careful."

Autumn felt relieved having Zach with her. To be honest, she had been apprehensive about going out to join the other BOG members, but she knew they might need her help. She had certainly been in slightly dangerous conditions at other times. If Zach was willing to walk her out to the investigation spot, she wasn't going to turn him down.

The forest was nearly silent as they found the path at the back of Cabin 2. They didn't hear any howls during their walk. As they neared the site, Autumn started to feel as if she was being watched. She had to pause a couple of times as Zach moved the flashlight from the path ahead of them to look for something off in the forest. She was happy to finally reach the dim lantern light that showed the BOG members sitting quietly in a circle, either writing on their keyboards or in their notebooks. They looked up as Autumn and Zach entered the clearing.

"Did you hear that?" Erica asked excitedly, jumping up to join them. "We didn't even have to do anything. Those howls came from somewhere to the east."

"Yes, I heard them," Autumn confirmed. She went right to a laptop that had been placed on a canvas chair, opened it, and started typing. She stopped long enough to look up at Zach. "I usually monitor the BOG website to see if anyone else is in our vicinity and has seen something. That's one of the reasons we knew we needed to come out here this weekend."

"Any activity?" Mike asked, leaning over Autumn's shoulder. Zach was surprised to feel a small twinge of jealousy.

"Yep. Two other reports on the live journal, indicating howls in Tahoma Valley. This is going to be an interesting night, guys."

Zach smiled. "Well, I'll leave you to your investigation."

"Are you sure?" Bill asked. "You don't want to stay?"

"I've had my share of monster-hunting evenings so far this year," Zach replied.

"At least wait a couple of minutes. I'm going to play one of our recordings and see if we get a response."

Zach decided there was no harm in waiting and watched as Nate and Bill took a voice recorder and a megaphone to the edge of the clearing. Bill called out "One, two, three," and then pressed play on the recorder. The sound that emerged made Zach cringe. The howls they just heard sounded nothing like the recording.

No response came. "Okay, I'll see you all sometime tomorrow," Zach said, and faced the dark trail. His flashlight gave him some comfort although every little rustle of bushes along the way made him uneasy. When he finally reached the edge of the clearing, a branch broke behind him. He broke out in a run and dashed for the door of the cabin. Certain that he could hear footsteps pounding behind him, he slammed the door and locked it.

It may have been his imagination in overdrive, but he thought he could hear something tapping on the door. He shook his head and stood quietly, careful to control his breathing. A gentle sigh came from the porch, and then one of the chairs was pushed over. Finally, thumps signified that whatever had followed him was gone.

"What the hell did I get into?" he muttered. He considered calling Brandon, then decided he needed to be alone with his thoughts.

He did turn the television on for some noise, and from time to time during the evening he glanced outside through the curtains. The light on the porch was strong, and there was nothing outside. Finally, he decided to go to bed. He was just pulling the covers up over his head when he heard excited voices and realized that Autumn and her friends had ended their investigation for the night.

After Zach left, the BOG members settled down. Autumn turned on the recorder to play a couple of calls while Nate and Mike stood quietly at the edge of the clearing. Every time they thought they heard a response, they recorded the time and the direction that the noise had come from.

After eleven, everyone admitted that they were tired. It had been a long day. "Let's wrap it up," Erica suggested. "We still have tomorrow and Sunday."

"Do you?" a voice called from the trail. Autumn and Tiffany screamed and turned around. Nate, Mike, and Bill immediately left what they were doing to stand in front of the women.

A flashlight kicked on and three young men stood at the trail head. "There's no Bigfoot around here," one of them said, his voice quiet but grim. "Why don't you all leave, or at least stop this foolishness of thinking you're going to find it?"

"People have seen something around here," Nate called out. "That's worth exploring, at least to us. Why is it a problem to you?"

"Because it seems like every few months, Tahoma Valley gets flooded by tourists who think they'll be making the next great discovery in human history," another man said. His tone was angry, but like the other men he didn't move from the trail. It seemed to Autumn that they were going to great lengths to not get too close to the BOG people.

"While the money is good, it disrupts our normal way of life," the first man said. "Either go back where you're from and leave us alone, or enjoy the rest of the weekend here and stop trying to draw out whatever may be hiding in these woods."

"So, there *is* something here!" Bill exclaimed.

The third man laughed, but didn't say anything else. A long silence extended between the two groups. It seemed that Erica was about to step forward when suddenly the same piercing howl they had heard earlier came through the air.

Everyone turned in different directions. Autumn shouted out "Look!" as she saw a dark shadowy figure on the opposite edge of the clearing.

Mike immediately took several pictures and then put the camera down. The figure disappeared when Autumn blinked, and she stared at the area in disbelief. She and her friends turned to notice that the men had already left, probably fleeing from the noise.

"The locals don't want us here?" Tiffany asked as they completed the takedown of their camp. "I think we have a reason to stay."

Everyone else agreed and decided to meet for breakfast the next day. Autumn wondered if she should go over and talk to Zach, but the lights in his cabin were off. She went up to her bed and cuddled under the comforter, thinking about the dark figure.

When Tony opened his eyes, he saw bright lights overhead. "Where am I?" he mumbled. He tried to move his arms and realized that one of them was bound tightly in bandages. A movement of his fingers and the resulting pain shooting up his wrist brought him back to reality with a gasp.

He tried to sit up and suddenly a man in a dark polo shirt, jeans, and a white coat appeared. "Hello, Mr. Simons. How are you feeling?"

Tony groaned and turned his head. He saw that he was in a small room with two other beds. The curtain around his bed was halfway open, and he could see into an empty hallway. "What happened? Where am I?"

"At the Tahoma Valley medical clinic. As for what happened, your friends and the sheriff were hoping that you'd be able to tell us that yourself."

Tony realized that his mind was blank. "I just remember being in the forest. It was dark." The doctor helped him sit up. "I think I hit my wrist on something, and then hit my head."

"I'm Dr. Smith," the man said. "Carson Smith. Your friends found you on the ground just outside the parking lot for the Valley Tavern. Did you have anything to drink tonight?"

"A couple of beers," Tony admitted. "I do remember we followed some people out to the parking lot because of some fuss over a man's truck." His mind started to clear. "He claimed that Bigfoot had stolen some fish from him."

"We hear stories like that a lot around here," Dr. Smith said. "Why did you go into the woods and your friends stayed behind?"

"I was looking for Bigfoot," Tony declared. "We were out in the forest all day, and I thought maybe it would still be around."

"Did you see it?" Dr. Smith asked. Tony studied the other man for a sign that he was being mocked, but the doctor's face remained serious.

"I don't remember," Tony realized. Frustration welled up inside him, and to his surprise he felt tears in his eyes. "I don't know what happened after I left the parking lot."

"Tony!" he heard Cal call from the doorway. "You're awake! Aaron!"

Both of his friends appeared by his bed. "You messed yourself up pretty bad," Cal said. "You have a broken wrist and your head was a bloody mess when we found you."

"Luckily there was a sheriff's deputy nearby," Aaron added. "We got you over here pretty quickly."

"Can I go home?" Tony asked, suddenly anxious to get out of the clinic. He wanted to be in familiar surroundings.

"We had to shave a small portion of your hair to put some stitches in, but other than the wrist and the cut I think you're in good shape," Dr. Smith said. Tony noticed one of the deputies from the tavern appear in the doorway. "Let me give you some instructions for what to do once you leave. You should definitely follow up with a doctor back in the city."

"I will," Tony whispered. His vision was clear, but he had a headache. He wanted to get back to the RV and sleep.

Dr. Smith stepped away. "What did you see?" Cal asked, concern in his face. "What happened?"

"I honestly can't remember anything beyond walking into the forest," Tony admitted. "Maybe if I have some time something will come back to me." He looked around the room. "Where's my camera?"

Aaron and Cal shrugged. "We didn't see it near you," Aaron said. "Were you taking a picture of something?"

Tony tried to search his mind. "Maybe? I feel like my arm was out and something hit it."

"Something?" asked the deputy. They turned. Reilly shook his head. "You're with those Bigfoot hunters, right?"

"We're part of BOG, yes," Cal answered. "There are a lot of separate teams in the area."

"Whatever you ran into, it wasn't Bigfoot," Reilly told them. "You all come out here a few times a year when people start seeing things in the woods. It's been going on for years, and no one has ever managed to come up with a Bigfoot carcass."

"Can we skip the lecture?" Tony groaned. "I'd just like some pain medication and to get out of here."

"I can help on both counts," Dr. Smith said, coming back into the room. He held up a small bottle. "Take one every four hours for the next couple of days, if needed. It's a mild pain reliever with no refills. Like I said, be sure to follow up with your own doctor. Here's a summary of what we did for you tonight and follow up instructions."

"Thank you," Tony said. Cal and Aaron helped him off the table. To his surprise, he was able to walk steadily. The pain in his head was already starting to subside, but he knew his wrist would be hurting for a long time.

Dr. Smith and Reilly watched the three men leave the clinic and didn't speak until they had driven away. "Anything on his camera?" Carson asked, removing the lab coat. He didn't like to wear it when there were no patients around.

"Just some pictures of fish. He must have dropped it before he could get anything else."

"I found a few small pieces of hair in his head wound. I collected them for the vault." Carson shook his head. "So, it was Bigfoot?"

"Yep. They're active again this weekend. The fish came from George's truck."

"My brother should know better than to leave dead animals in the bed of his truck around here," Carson said sharply. He glanced up at the clock. "You think those guys are going to be trouble for us?"

"Not anymore. There were a lot of people out near the end of town today, and most of them seem to have left after a day trip. That happens. They'll hear on their online forum that people are seeing Bigfoot, and they'll decide to make a day out of it. There are others who are more devoted and come out for the weekend."

"Hopefully George is getting some sleep tonight," Carson said. "It's the ten-year anniversary this weekend."

"He was talking to someone named Zach Larson at the Valley Tavern yesterday. He's the host of a show called…"

"*Creature Hunt*," Carson finished. "I've seen it. What's his story?"

"Claims he's out here on vacation. Mitzi's loosely keeping an eye on him. He's formed an attachment to one of the BOG teams. I don't know what they're up to, but I think your brother might get a visit from them tomorrow."

"Damn," Carson swore. "Okay. Where's Tony's camera?"

"In the vault, where we keep everything else that gets dropped during Bigfoot hunts like this," Reilly said. "Let me have the hair and I'll put it away, then erase the pictures and bring the camera to their campsite tomorrow."

"If that's all he got on film, it's probably better if he gets the camera back," Carson agreed. "Well, I'm going to go see if I can get some sleep tonight. See you around, Reilly."

"Have a good night, Carson."

Carson disappeared down the hall. Reilly sent a message to Joey about Tony and his friends, then walked out into the crisp night. He had heard a lot of howls and other calls this evening. Mitzi had told him the BOG members at her resort were responsible for some of them, and he knew a few of the men from town had gone out to see them. All they could do was keep warning people away from trying to find Bigfoot. The townspeople knew what dangers the monster could bring to humans when it didn't want to be found.

CHAPTER 12

On Saturday morning, Zach got out of bed and opened the curtains. He realized that he could see a very small part of the shelter from his window up here. He decided that he should tell the BOG group about it. They were here to look for Bigfoot, and since he had knowledge about a phenomenon associated with the creature, it was time to pass that along to them. He was starting to feel like he was caught in the middle of an episode of his show.

He took a shower and dressed, then found the brochures on the kitchen table as he started the coffee maker. He looked through them again. The caves in question were at the end of what appeared to be a dirt road stemming off from the highway. It wouldn't be impossible for someone to go out and find them without the map, but Zach wondered how many people had made the attempt.

He looked at the phone number and saw it that it was after nine. Surely George would be up by now. He used the phone in the cabin. After three rings, a gruff voice that Zach recognized said "Hello?"

"Hi, my name is Zach Larson. Is this George?"

"Yes, it is." George cleared his throat. "I see you got the clue I left you, Zach."

"Is there something you'd like to talk about?"

"Yeah, I think so. Did you see what happened to my truck last night?"

"I was there in the parking lot with you and the cops, remember?"

George laughed. "Sometimes I don't want to remember. One of my friends ended up driving me out of there last night." He paused. "How about we talk this afternoon, maybe around one o'clock? You can come here. I'm not in the mood to drive around with the town filled with Bigfoot hunters today."

"Sure. Where do you live?"

George gave him directions to a house on the opposite

side of Tahoma Valley from the cabins. "If you want to bring someone with you, you can."

"Anyone in particular?"

"I only want to tell this story once. Any way you want to record it or write it down is fine with me, and anyone you want to bring is okay, as well."

"Thank you, George."

"See you at one, Zach."

Zach poured his coffee and smiled. He had been hoping for a vacation, but was again starting to get caught up in the search for a monster. His smile faded slightly as he wondered where today would lead. Mitzi had mentioned speaking to an older man named Stan who had lived here a long time. If he was going to bring Autumn with him, as she had suggested, he should probably also take her along to see George. No doubt she'd be interested in his story.

Seeing that the shades in Cabin 2 were still down, he walked over to the general store and found Mitzi behind the counter. "Hi, Zach!" she called out. "Anything I can get you?"

He looked around a couple of aisles of snacks as he answered. "Hopefully an interview today with that man Stan you told me about."

"I'll call him this morning," Mitzi promised. "Any particular time?"

"If he's free mid-afternoon, please let him know I'd like to stop by then. I have a couple of other places to be before that." He settled on beef jerky, potato chips, and a couple of bottles of pop. "Did you hear those howls last night?"

"I heard several. Some of them were that Bigfoot group out in the woods. Some of them, though…" she shook her head as she handed him his change. "Seems like this time of year the woods around here are more active."

"Do you have a big group of people hunting Bigfoot here every June?"

"Yep. Don't know why. Maybe there are just more people starting to come up here in June so supposed sightings go way up, which leads to groups like BOG setting out one more time in hopes of finding they evidence they want." Mitzi sighed. "Not that we don't appreciate the business around here, but it's better when we just get the normal tourists, especially around Independence Day. That's a fun crowd."

"I bet it is." Zach left the store and headed back to his cabin. He saw Autumn just pulling up the front window shade and went to the door. She opened it before he could knock.

"You won't believe what happened after you left last night," she said, coming out onto the porch to talk to him. "Three of the locals came by and warned us to stop what we were doing, saying we'd be better off just enjoying the town for a few days."

"Did that worry you?" Zach asked. He had encountered that before during the filming of a few episodes. He had learned that the people in the areas around the supposed monster sightings often grew tired of being asked about the monsters.

"A little. I think it means they know something is actually around here."

"I see." Zach proceeded to tell her about his phone call with George that morning. "Would you like to come along with me to see George and then this guy Stan? I have no idea what they can tell us, but as long as I'm in the area I thought I'd take the time to talk to them."

"That would be great!" Autumn exclaimed. "I'll let Erica and the others know that I'll be out this afternoon."

Zach hesitated, then looked across at his cabin. "Your whole group might be interested in something else that I found yesterday."

"What would that be?" Autumn asked. Erica opened the door behind them and blinked against the bright sunlight.

"Are we having breakfast?" she asked quietly.

"Zach was just mentioning something that we might want to see," Autumn replied.

Zach smiled. "It's not going anywhere. Why don't you get

your group together and meet at my cabin around eleven?"

Autumn checked her watch to see that it was nearly ten already. "Sounds good. See you then." She went back into the cabin with Erica, discussing their meal options.

"Can you believe this?" Bill breathed as he stared at the branch structure.

"I've been waiting many years to see something like this," Mike admitted, taking pictures. He shook his head. "I can't say this wasn't built by humans, but I think we all know it had to have been built by something with hands."

Zach, sitting on a stump off to the side, silently agreed. He had felt from the first time he had seen the structure that something out here was using it as a temporary shelter. He didn't believe that a human, even a hermit trying to keep away from civilization, would take the time to build something this elaborate out of just branches and parts of nearby shrubs.

Nate walked around it a couple of times in silence. "When did you first notice this?" he asked Zach.

"Yesterday morning. I saw it from behind the cabin and crossed the creek, looked inside and took pictures, and then followed that trail." He pointed to the opening in the tree line. "Turns out it connects to a larger trail that leads to a popular sighting spot down near the highway."

"Hey, we were there yesterday!" Autumn called from the creek. She and Erica were looking for foot prints while being very careful where they were stepping.

"Did any of you notice this over here?" Tiffany called from several yards away. Everyone turned to look, but they couldn't see her.

"Where are you?" Nate called back, concern in his voice.

"Up here." Zach saw branches moving roughly ten feet above the ground. "Mike, do you have a couple of plastic containers? There's something here you might want to collect."

Zach, Mike, and Nate all followed the sound of her voice.

They found themselves at the bottom of a roughly cut ladder that led to a small observation platform. Tiffany looked down at them and made a face.

"I think something either left behind some rotting food or threw it up," she said, placing her feet on the ladder.

"Be careful," Nate cautioned. He held her leg as she descended back down to the ground. "How did you find this?"

"I went looking for prints away from the water," she said. "I didn't find those, but I did find this platform."

Zach studied it. "I think this was probably built by a hunter." He climbed up on the ladder, appreciating the sturdiness. When he reached the top of the platform, Mike joined him and frowned at the mess on the side. "I don't think this is from Bigfoot," he whispered to Zach.

Zach nodded in agreement. He looked through the trees. From here, he could see Autumn and Erica by the creek, Bill standing in the doorway of the shelter, and part of the resort. He wondered how many times someone had come up here and watched the people across the creek. Just from his vantage point here he noticed the people in the next group of cabins playing volleyball in an open field, and Mitzi walking from cabin to cabin. Seeing her made him check his watch. There was still time to stay here with the BOG group.

Nate and Mike chatted at the bottom of the ladder. Zach saw Tiffany join Autumn and Erica by the creek. He turned around, and suddenly realized that something else was watching the girls as well.

In a dark stand of trees and ferns just fifty feet away from the hunting platform, Zach saw a tall shape stand up. When a large hand pushed aside one of the ferns, his heart started racing. He sat down on the platform and leaned over the edge. Nate saw him and Zach motioned for the two men to be quiet. They stopped talking, and he quietly pointed to the ferns where the hand was clearly visible.

Zach heard them both suck in their breath. Mike's hand was shaking as he tried to aim his camera in the direction of the ferns. Just as he started taking pictures, the hand disappeared and branches shook as the creature moved away from them. Mike started after it, but Nate caught the back of his windbreaker and shook his head.

Zach quietly climbed down from the platform, shaking. During the filming of the show, there had been times when he had thought he had seen the elusive creatures they were hunting. This was the first time, though, that he had actually seen something that he believed was a Bigfoot. It made him even more curious about the shelter and what was using it, and for how long.

"It was watching the women," he whispered to Nate and Mike. "Let's get out of here. I don't think it likes us being in its territory."

"Agreed. We have no idea what direction it was headed anyway," Nate replied.

"These pictures look like every other supposed picture of something that's supposed to be Bigfoot," Mike complained as they walked to rejoin the group. "Lame."

"Find anything?" Autumn asked as the men came back to the shelter.

"Not really," Mike said. "Although there was something moving around." Before Nate and Zach could stop him, he showed the pictures to the women.

"Is that a hand?" Erica asked.

"Maybe," Tiffany said. "This next one is just a brown blur. It could be anything."

"Whatever it is didn't want us to see it," Autumn said, and everyone else nodded in agreement.

Zach looked at his watch. "Autumn, we should leave soon if we want to talk to George."

"Oh, right."

"Do you have time for lunch?" Nate asked. "They serve some hot food at the general store."

They agreed to meet back at the store. Everyone else crossed the creek, but Zach stayed behind at the shelter for a couple of moments. He hoped that the lack of activity would bring out whatever creature was lurking in the bushes.

"I know you're here," he said. He took a branch and knocked it twice against the nearest tree. This time it didn't take long for the response to come. Zach nodded. They were getting closer to finding Bigfoot.

CHAPTER 13

George opened the front door and watched as Zach parked his car behind the familiar truck. Autumn studied the man as she gathered up her backpack to get out of the car. "I don't think I've seen this guy yet."

"I met him at the Valley Tavern on Thursday," Zach said. "Although I saw him briefly last night. He's very nervous about something, so please let me take the lead on this."

"It's your show," Autumn said, and winked.

Zach smiled and opened the door. George waved to them as they approached the porch. "Hi, Zach. And what's your name, ma'am?"

"Autumn Hunter," she said, shaking his hand. "Thank you for letting me come along to hear your story."

"You're welcome," George said. He invited them in to a comfortable, well-used living room. It was neater than Zach had been expecting. "I cleaned up a bit this morning," George said, seeing the look on Zach's face. "I don't entertain much."

He offered them beverages, and they accepted coffee. As George was in the kitchen preparing it, Autumn set up a video camera on a tripod, trying to keep it low and out of their way. Zach pulled out a notebook, prepared to take handwritten notes. He preferred to do this when meeting with witnesses for the show, as it appeared to set them more at ease than simply having a recording device watching them. More than one had told him that they felt he was taking them seriously when he wrote down what he needed to know from them. Thinking about this now, Zach wondered if anything he had ever noted down had actually contributed something important to the narrator's script.

George came back in with a tray filled with a coffee pot, mugs, sugar and milk, and some cookies. He placed the food and drink on the beautifully carved coffee table and they chatted about the town as they prepared their beverages.

After Autumn and Zach had each taken a cookie, George

cleared his throat. "You're with Bigfoot Online Group?" he asked Autumn.

"I'm part of that forum, yes. There's not really an official leader. We're just a collection of people interested in Bigfoot. The website contains sightings, any photographic evidence that people collect, sightings in other states, and a chat room that can sometimes get very heated."

"I bet. Bigfoot is a pretty controversial topic."

"Not just Bigfoot," Zach put in. "Really, any cryptid has its own community that wants to believe in it and detractors who want to disprove that any such creature exists."

George smiled sadly. "Until about ten years ago, I would never have known the words cryptid or cryptozoology. Luckily, I enjoy using the library and I needed to know what was going on with me." He took a drink from his cup. "And you, Zach, must sometimes getting tired of hearing stories like this."

"I'm always interested in hearing about monsters," Zach said. "From people who have seen them as well as those who don't believe in them."

"How about people who have had physical contact with a Bigfoot?" George asked.

"Is that what happened to you?" Autumn asked. She took a moment to push the recording button on the camera and made sure that George was in the frame.

"Yes. And I've regretted it every day since."

"Why don't you start at the beginning?" Zach suggested. He leaned back into the couch and crossed his legs, propping his notebook on his leg.

"I was a couple of years out of high school, taking some classes at a community college. My friends and I were a bunch of party guys. I guess in some ways we still are," he said to Zach. "You saw us at the tavern the other night. We're a bit beyond being wild and crazy, but still young enough to enjoy good times on a late night out."

Zach nodded. "You were just getting settled into a life you wanted."

"Yep. My dad and my brother and I were all still living in the house down on Forest Hill Road."

"Forest Hill Road?" Autumn put in. "We're meeting with a man named Stan on that road after we're finished here."

"That's my dad," George said. "You'll enjoy meeting him." He paused, and looked out the window. He seemed to tense up for a minute, then relaxed again. He turned back to Zach and Autumn.

"My best friend back then was Harry Pike. One Friday night, he and I were hanging out at my dad's house. We had a few drinks in us and were sitting out near the fire pit in the side yard. It was the night of the summer solstice, and still light enough around ten o'clock that we were just able to make out the outline of a huge figure crossing the gravel road a few hundred feet away from us."

"Were you both facing the road?" Autumn asked.

"Yep. I pointed it out to Harry and he got excited. If you grow up around here, you're always being told to avoid certain parts of the forest because of Bigfoot. I know it's different up in the cities, but out here people are usually believed when they say that they've seen it."

Zach thought about that, and nodded in agreement. He had seen it a lot in his interviews for *Creature Hunt.* People who lived near forests or empty grassland areas, people who hunted or fished often, or even just hiking enthusiasts spent a lot of time in the forest. They saw animals and observed their behavior. Even though he was supposed to remain open to the testimony of all witnesses, he invariably trusted the accounts of people like George.

"So, since we were young and stupid, we decided to investigate. We got flashlights and set out down the road. Dad and Carson were gone that night, so there was no one to convince us that this was a stupid idea." He sighed and drank some coffee. "We came to the parking lot for that particular hiking area. Back then the signs for the caves were prominent out on the highway and also down at the parking lot. Dad had quite a bit of traffic going down that way during the summer.

"Well, we had just reached the trail head when we heard the howling. It was followed by what I would call a couple of whoops, and then that pattern repeated twice more. We started down that trail, but I was shaking and I could see that Harry had become nervous. Both of our flashlight beams were bouncing around from the trail in front of us to the trees around us. We had gone about half a mile when we started hearing branches breaking and bushes shaking off to our right. We stopped, and the sounds stopped as well." George swallowed and stared off into the distance.

Autumn opened her mouth to ask a question, but Zach shook his head at her. She frowned. Zach settled back into his chair. He knew if they didn't let George get this story out at his own pace, he might never get up the courage to speak about it to them again.

"We kept walking, and whatever was following us kept making noise. It was there, and it wanted us to know it was there. The caves are about a mile in from the parking lot, and as we reached them it was finally dark enough around us to ensure that the only light available was from our flashlights.

"Well, there we were at the entrance. Finally, the noise in the forest stopped, and Harry whispered 'Let's go see what's out there.'

'What about the cave?' I asked.

'I think whatever we wanted to find in there is out here,' he said.

"So, we went around the cave entrance. There's a path, not very well laid out, that leads down from the upper trail in that area. We walked past it and found our way to an area that seemed to be near the back of the cave. There's a clearing there, and it was there that we saw it." George closed his eyes. "Our flashlights hit it at the same time. Bigfoot. It was around nine feet tall, with grayish-brown hair over its whole body. It was standing next to a stump, and on that stump was a smaller creature, this one with pure brown hair. The big one was probably at least eight hundred pounds. They looked like they were waiting for us to do something.

"That's one thing you need to take away from this. These creatures are intelligent. Their eyes looked human, and we could see some mix of both ape and human in their facial structure. The big one let out the same howl we had heard earlier, and the whooping sound that answered it came from the smaller one.

"I don't know when Harry had grabbed a knife, but right then he brought it out. I didn't see it on him when we left, but maybe he came over armed hoping for something like this to happen. All I know is I saw him hold it in front of him. We stood still for a long minute, and then suddenly the little one stood up from the stump and ran to us. That startled Harry, and he lunged forward and slashed the little one's arm as it passed us, presumably to go back to the cave.

"The noise that monster made still wakes me up from nightmares. And then the large one strode over to us. It only took him a couple steps to get to Harry. And then…" George's voice broke. "He picked up my friend and threw him. Harry landed against a nearby tree, and the force of it snapped his spine. His head cracked against a pile of rocks as his body landed. Harry was dead."

George placed his face in his hands, fighting back tears. Zach's heart was racing. He saw a tear fall down Autumn's face.

"I ran. The path was clear and I turned off my flashlight to hopefully avoid detection. The Bigfoot watched me leave. I passed the cave entrance and didn't pause to look back. I ran as fast as I could. When I reached the trail head and the parking lot, I finally stopped. There was something that was following my path, breaking branches almost as swiftly as I was running, but it stopped when I reached the open lot.

"I sat down on a rock to catch my breath. I turned on my flashlight again. I played it over the bushes and saw eyes reflecting at me from eight or nine feet off the ground. It was then that the sheriff's car pulled up."

Zach found his voice again. "Was it Reilly?"

"Yep. He had heard the howls and was out on patrol. Even

back then, June seemed to be an active time for Bigfoot sightings. The moment his headlights appeared, the Bigfoot disappeared from sight."

"He drove me home, and Dad and Carson were there. I managed to get the story out, and Reilly gathered his deputies together to go check out the cave and retrieve Harry's body. The Bigfoot must have decided that they had enough contact with people, because those men saw nothing. Harry's body was brought out, I went to tell his family that I was sorry, and his funeral was a few days later."

"Did you tell his parents the truth about what killed him?" Autumn asked.

"Yes. I don't know if they believed me or not. I guess maybe they thought he and I were so drunk that he had fallen from the upper trail. But I didn't want to lie to them."

"Are the Pikes still in the area?" Autumn asked.

"No. They moved away the next year. A few months after Harry's death, once a lot of the excitement had died down, my dad went to the town council and recommended that the caves be taken off the tourism maps. They agreed, and printed new ones the next year."

"Do you know why this is a time of year when Bigfoot is more active?" Autumn asked.

"No idea. I don't know if there's a connection to the summer solstice, or if it was just coincidence that they were hanging around outside the cave that night."

Zach shook his head to clear his thoughts. "Have you ever seen them since?"

"A few times. Every now and then I'll be sitting here watching a baseball or football game and look up to see a hairy face staring at me through my window. There are some incidents around my yard, even with my truck. You saw one of those last night. I figure they blame me for Harry hurting the young one, and are trying to warn me to stay away from them."

"That makes sense," Autumn said. She turned off her recorder.

George stared blankly at her. "You think they want us to stay away, and yet you're trying to find them?"

"As you pointed out, not everyone outside of areas like this believes in Bigfoot. If we can get hair and blood samples, and definitive pictures, maybe we can get it classified as an actual animal and give it some protection, instead of leaving it as a cryptid."

"I've seen enough of Bigfoot to last me a lifetime," George said.

Zach nodded. "I understand. Thank you for taking the time to speak to us."

"My dad knows the whole story, so don't be afraid to ask him for his opinion of us. 'Young idiots' is probably how he'll describe me and Harry, but after ten years of distance from the events I agree with him."

"We're looking forward to meeting him," Autumn said. "Thank you, George. I know this wasn't easy for you."

"You're welcome." He saw them to the door and watched as they got into their car and drove away.

When he shut the door and turned around, he saw it. Bigfoot stood outside his window, not quite close enough to leave any marks on the glass. "Go away," he shouted. The monster backed up and disappeared into the bushes.

George ran to the phone and frantically dialed the first number that came to mind. "Carson, I think those Bigfoot hunters are going down to the cave this evening. We have to stop them or someone else might die."

CHAPTER 14

By the time Zach and Autumn pulled up in front of Stanley Smith's log cabin, it was late afternoon. Autumn looked around nervously as they got out of the car. "Is it just me, or do you also feel like you're being watched?" she asked as they climbed the stairs to the covered wrap-around porch.

Zach nodded. "Yep. I've been feeling that way since we turned down this road. Hard to say at this point if it's humans or animals keeping track of us."

"This weekend isn't turning out like I expected," Autumn confessed. "I thought we'd be sitting around and chatting with other BOG members and simply going where we thought we'd find Bigfoot."

"The townspeople are afraid," a deep voice said from behind them. Zach immediately pulled Autumn to his side and turned. An older man stood close to the fire pit George had mentioned, an axe in his hand. His hair was white and cut short, and he wore jeans and a dark t-shirt. The emblem of a big city police department was on the shirt, and Zach remembered that Stanley Smith was retired law enforcement.

"Mr. Smith?" he asked. He felt Autumn squeeze his arm gently, and he let go of her. "My name is Zach Larson. This is Autumn Hunter. Mitzi sent us to talk to you."

The man nodded. "Stanley Smith. Please call me Stan." He saw Autumn's gaze resting on the axe. "Sorry. I was out cutting some wood for my stove. Nights can still sometimes get cold around here." He walked over to a nearby stump and swung the axe down into it. Returning to the porch, he opened the door and gestured at them. "Mitzi called to say you'd be here. Please come in."

'Thank you," Autumn said. She marched right in to the cabin. Zach followed, taking a last look down the road before Stan closed the door.

"Are you part of that online group that's here?" Stan asked, gesturing for them to sit down. The cabin was bigger than it had looked and very nicely furnished. Family pictures adorned a mantel above a gas fireplace along one wall. A wood stove sat in a far corner near the doorway to what Zach presumed was the kitchen. A hallway behind the living room wall led to a couple of bedrooms and a bathroom. A large television sat in another corner of the living room, right across from the soft couch where Stanley perched on the edge of his seat.

"I am," Autumn said. "We came out here because we had been hearing of more activity and sightings than usual. We've been trying to collect evidence all weekend, but it seems like whatever we've encountered has been just beyond our reach."

"No surprise there. If someone was constantly trying to stalk you, you'd probably try to stay hidden, too." He offered them coffee, and they accepted. "What about you, Zach? Why are you out here?"

"I'm the host of *Creature Hunt*, a show that searches for cryptids, or unknown animals. Bigfoot is probably the biggest legend out of all the creatures I've investigated. I came to Mitzi's resort for a weekend of relaxation while the show is on a break, but I met Autumn and her friends and got caught up in their investigation."

"That's understandable. Even just talking about Bigfoot and the stories around it can bring people who have opposite viewpoints together. Each side may come away thinking the other is crazy, but they'll discuss it all the same."

"Stan, do you know what's going on here? Is there a reason why people might be seeing Bigfoot more frequently lately?"

Stan sat back on the couch and took a sip from his cup, appearing to consider her question. "It's the summer solstice tonight. Strange things have always happened in this area of the mountain around this time of year."

"How many Bigfoot are there?" Autumn asked in a whisper.

"I don't know. It's not like we can take a census." Stan chuckled. "They stay near the cave down the hill from here.

About three miles further down the road, there's a parking lot lined with logs and gates to keep people off the trails. Not many people find their way down here. The locals know to avoid it and they direct tourists to other areas closer to the lake and the campgrounds."

"What would we find if we went down there?" Zach asked.

"You'd find the evidence that you're looking for."

Autumn sat up. "Then what are we waiting for?"

Stan shook his head. "Why would you want to put yourself and your friends in danger? There are creatures down there that are large, strong, not very friendly, and want to be left alone."

"But this could be our one chance," Autumn argued.

"These creatures don't care about your chance, Autumn."

"Stan, have you ever been down to the caves?" Zach asked. The old man looked out the window, and Zach thought that he was about to cry.

"Yes," he said, struggling to keep his voice even. "And I saw enough to know to never venture down that way again."

"What about other people in town?"

"My son and a few of his friends." Stan took another sip of coffee. "Have you talked to George?"

"Yes. I know that he thinks a Bigfoot is stalking him right now." Zach paused. "He also told us about his friend Harry's death."

Stan nodded. "George was once a lot like you, Autumn. He had heard about the Bigfoot from other people in the area and wanted to find them. Every now and then he and some of his friends went Bigfoot hunting." He smiled sadly. "They finally made it down to the caves and tragedy followed. Now, every now and then, Bigfoot comes to find him. It's been a hard thing for him to live with. He left Tahoma Valley once and was worried that they'd find him in the city. He came back here for the safety of being around people who know him."

Autumn sighed. She closed her eyes. "I would give

anything to finally be able to present the world with the evidence that this legend exists."

"Be careful what you wish for," Stan warned. He looked out the window again and abruptly sat up. "Both of you, stay still and very quiet."

Autumn opened her mouth, but Zach shook his head. They stayed still, waiting for something to happen. Stan looked around the room and very quickly retrieved another axe from the corner by the wood stove. He then tiptoed over to Autumn and whispered "Do you really want to see a Bigfoot?"

She nodded. Zach suddenly felt very nervous. His camera and cell phone were in the car, because he had not expected to need them during this visit. He could tell by the look on her face that she regretted leaving her phone behind as well. He shrugged at her. "At least we'll have a story to tell," he whispered as they stood and joined Stan at the door.

"Hush," Stan said quietly. He opened the front door. Zach leaned to the side and saw nothing beyond the doorway.

"What did you see?" he asked.

"Something in the trees near the end of the driveway. Are you ready for some possible action?"

"Yes," Autumn replied forcefully. She pushed Zach to the side and went out the front door.

"Autumn, wait," Stan said. However, she was already down the stairs and heading across the gravel. Zach followed her more cautiously, wondering what was going through her head. He was more than willing to let Stan control the situation. It appeared, though, that Autumn had other plans.

As Autumn walked towards the road her heart started beating faster. Perhaps this was the moment when she would finally see a dream come true. She stopped several feet past the car and turned to face a thick stand of trees. A large shape came into focus and stepped out into the clearing, and she gasped.

It was over nine feet tall, with graying brown hair matted and twisted over its massive body. Its face had some human qualities, but there was enough resemblance to an ape that Autumn knew it was more animal than human. The enormous size of its feet that gave the creature its name made her shudder. She stared at it in silence, trying to figure out if she could somehow communicate with this creature.

Bigfoot took a step forward and let out a roar. Surprised, Autumn took a few steps back. Zach and Stan rushed across the clearing just as the animal grabbed Autumn's arm and pulled her forward. "No!" she screamed, suddenly frightened. This was not how she had envisioned her first encounter with Bigfoot.

"Let her go," Stan shouted, as if the creature could understand him. Remarkably, Bigfoot turned at the sound of his voice and shook his head. He roared again.

"Okay, then," Stan replied calmly. As Zach and Autumn both watched in horror, Stan raised his axe and brought it down on the monster's arm.

The creature howled in pain and released Autumn. She ran straight to Zach and threw her arms around him, sobbing. He held her and watched over her shoulder as the animal held its arm and glared at Stan. Stan took another swing with the axe and missed, but the creature took the hint. Bleeding from its wound, it ran back into the forest. They could hear branches breaking and the distinctive thumps of its huge feet running down the hill into the valley.

"Well, that will stir them up," Stan said. He turned to Zach and Autumn. "Are the two of you okay?"

"Oh my God, evidence!" Autumn said when she turned away from Zach and noticed the blood on the ground.

"Seriously?" Zach asked as she opened the car and dug through her backpack. "Autumn, we need to get out of Tahoma Valley."

"We can't leave now," she countered. "We need to get down to that cave." She pulled out a small vial and kneeled on the ground. "There's blood here. We can bring it to a lab." After collecting some of the blood, she retrieved her camera and took pictures. Now that she was out of danger and able to document her sighting, she was back in good spirits.

Zach noticed strands of hair on the axe. He collected that in his own container and placed it in his bag. "There's a lot of dirt mixed in with that blood," Zach said. He turned to Stan. "What do you think we should do now?"

"I agree with you. I think you should leave and not look back. They will be down in that cave tonight, and now that one of them is wounded they'll be on the lookout for danger. Any normal person would take that as a warning."

"I'm not a normal person," Autumn shot back. "I mean, I am most of the time. But we're so close now to proving the existence of Bigfoot! I'm going to call the rest of the group to get them down here so we can hike down to that cave. How far is it from the parking lot?"

Stan remained silent. She walked up to him and looked him in the eyes. "I'm going whether you think I should or not. I'll wander through the woods all night, if I have to."

The old man sighed. "Come back inside. I'll draw a map for you."

"Thank you!" Autumn grinned. Stan remained grim and walked back into his house. She turned to Zach and realized that he, too, was not smiling. "Zach, don't you think we should do this while we're here?"

"No," he replied firmly. "I just watched you almost get carried off by a Bigfoot. I think that's all I want to see of it."

"That was just the beginning. I need the others here for credibility in our sighting and to take backup photos and possibly distract them long enough to collect hair and skin."

Zach was amazed at Autumn's persistence. In one way he admired it, but he was growing weary of her enthusiasm. "Autumn, what are you going to do if there's more than one Bigfoot in the cave? Do you have any weapons? Anything to protect yourself?"

"Do you take weapons along on your investigations?" Autumn replied as she led the way out through Stan's door. "We'll be fine."

"I always have something that can be used to protect us.

My flashlight can become a weapon, and I carry a taser that will at least allow me and my crew time to get away. We think of that before we go charging into what could be a dangerous situation."

"Mike and Bill will think of something," Autumn said with an assurance that Zach did not share.

Stan motioned for them to come over to the kitchen table. "Here's my house, and here's the road that you drove in on. You turn right out of my driveway and go three miles. You'll find the parking lot. There are a couple of paths there. One leads to a lower elevation and is a direct route to the front of the cave. The other will keep you a bit higher on the hill and has a line of sight down to the path below. At some point there is a trail from the upper path to the lower one, not well marked. Whichever route you want to take is up to you."

Zach looked at the clock. "It's almost six. We better return to the resort and come back later." He shook Stan's hand. "Will you be okay tonight out here, sir?"

"I think so. Reilly and his partner drive by here most nights when they're on duty. My sons come to check on me now and then, too. George will probably be staying in his house tonight, though."

Zach shuddered at the thought. "Is there any way to put a stop to it?"

"Not that I know of. They're pretty intelligent, those creatures. They remember what's done to them. They seem to have the capabilities of a human brain with the brute strength of an animal." He looked directly at Autumn. "Remember that. You're not hunting teddy bears."

"I know," she said, and for just a brief moment wondered if she was doing the right thing. "I'll let my friends know that it's a serious situation. No one has to come tonight if they don't want to."

"Good." Stan watched them get into the car, then shut his door.

"What are we waiting for?" Autumn asked brightly. "Let's head back and get our team together."

"I guess I'm part of the team now, too," Zach replied, and softly smiled. "Okay, let's go."

CHAPTER 15

"What?" Erica exclaimed after Autumn had finished telling her friends what she had seen and experienced. Zach had parked in front of his house and told her that he'd meet them around nine o'clock to go down to the caves.

"It was intense, Erica. This creature actually touched me. It held my arms. I think it was going to pull me into the woods, but then Stan hit it with an axe."

"Please tell me it bled," Nate said. Tiffany looked at him in dismay.

"Yes," Autumn confirmed. She pulled the vial out of her backpack. "I got a sample."

Mike and Bill grabbed the vial from her and stared at it in amazement. "Where should we keep this?" Bill asked. "We need it to be intact to take to a lab."

"I'm keeping it right here in my evidence kit," Autumn replied, taking it back from them. "And the kit is coming with us to the cave tonight."

"Are you sure?" Mike asked. "What if something happens to it."

"Nothing will happen. I just want to keep everything together. When we have a chance to get hair and skin samples, I'll need the kit with me."

"What time are we going down to these caves?" Nate asked.

"Zach said he'd be back around nine."

Erica shook her head. "It's not going to be easy, but I do admire your level of planning."

Tiffany moved to the kitchen. "We brought a casserole over. I'll start getting it ready for dinner. You'll all need your strength for tonight."

Nate followed her to the kitchen. "What do you mean 'you all'? Aren't you coming with us?"

Autumn was right behind him. She was curious to hear Tiffany's response. "Is there something I can do that doesn't involve a night hike to a cave filled with monsters?" Tiffany asked with an edge to her voice.

Nate moved closer to her and glanced at Autumn. She took the hint and went back to the living room, allowing her friend and his fiancée to continue their disagreement in private. Erica, Mike, and Bill were talking about what they could expect. Bill had Stan's map in his hand and examined it for a long time. "I think we should take the direct approach," he said. "We can sneak down this path quietly."

"I agree," Erica said. She went to Autumn's open laptop and refreshed the current page. "No one else seems to be talking about this on BOG. In fact, it's been rather quiet since this morning."

"Eerily quiet," Mike added. "It's like suddenly no one has seen anything at all."

"Maybe they didn't," Erica said.

Bill smiled. "I ran into a couple of people in town who know Tony Simons. Apparently, he went out into the woods by the Valley Tavern last night and something knocked him out cold. He's okay, but he and his friends are staying close to their campsite. Since he's often the one stirring up sightings, maybe people decided to leave or just give up for the weekend after not seeing anything."

Tiffany walked into the dining room and started setting the table. Nate came back into the living room. "Are those body cameras charged?"

"Yes," Bill said. "But they're back at the campground, in the trailer."

"Tiffany has agreed to come with us tonight, but she won't leave the parking lot. Instead, she is going to stay in the car and be prepared to call for help."

"Let's go get the cameras," Bill said. "How long until dinner?"

"About thirty minutes," Tiffany said from across the room.

Mike got out his keys. "See you in a few." He left, and Autumn walked over to Tiffany.

"Thank you for agreeing to go with us," she said. "I know

this seems crazy to you."

"I just don't want anything to happen to Nate," Tiffany replied. "Or any of you. The first sign that something is going wrong, and you better come back. I'll also have my cell so I will call the local sheriff's office if I think I need to do so."

"That sounds like a good idea," Autumn said. As the scent of the hamburger and tater tot casserole filled the cabin, she stepped over to the window. Zach was in his cabin and moving around. She could barely make out his shadow behind the curtains.

"Someone please tell me I'm crazy," Zach said to the empty cabin. Usually when he uttered those words, he had a team of people around him trying to convince him that he was not crazy, that he had actually seen something. There was no such help tonight.

He watched as the frozen dinner turned around in the microwave. "That was a Bigfoot! BIGFOOT!" he shouted to no one. He looked around just to be sure that no one was lurking at any of the windows. "And I'm actually going to follow these people out to a cave tonight to go to its home. To an area where a real person died." He shook his head. "Someone please tell me I'm crazy."

No response came. He stirred the small tray of macaroni and cheese and placed it down next to the small bowl of vegetables he had also heated in the microwave. Opening the fridge, he briefly considered a can of beer but decided he'd need a level head tonight. He pulled out a can of soda and sat down to his dinner, wondering what Autumn was eating tonight.

He had been terrified for her this afternoon. He wondered where this zealousness of hers came from. He had seen it before when people were talking about monsters, but Bigfoot always seemed to evoke more passion from people. Maybe because it was one of the more frequently sighted creatures, and seemed to be all over the world and known by many different names.

Zach had spoken to an anthropologist for the state of Washington once about legends of Bigfoot. She said that she had seen paintings in caves that featured a tall hairy man, and that stories about the creature existed among several cultures that had been so far apart it would have been nearly impossible to share those legends. She believed it had been, and still was, a real animal just like the birds and bears also drawn in the cave.

Zach finished his dinner and decided to have a chocolate bar for dessert. He pulled his favorite one out of the grocery bag and opened it. Now was the time to make the decision. Would he bow out and let the BOG members fend for themselves? Or would he join them and let this be the most real episode of monster hunting he had ever experienced?

The decision was easy.

CHAPTER 16

Shortly before nine, Zach walked over to Cabin 1 and knocked on the door. Autumn answered and gestured for him to come in. She was wearing jeans and a long-sleeve light gray shirt. She was carrying a jacket that she placed on the arm of the couch. Zach noticed that there were two pockets on the jacket chest that were covered with clear plastic.

"What are those for?" he asked.

"The camera," she replied.

The rest of the team moved into the living room from the dining room, where they had been talking about their positions for the night. "Hi, Zach," Nate said. "Would you like to hear what we've decided to do?"

"Of course."

"We'll drive down there in two cars, yours and Mike's. When we get to the parking lot on this map, we'll park off to this side here." He pointed to an area that was right along a fence. "Mike, Bill, and Tiffany will stay in the lot. Tiffany is going to keep her phone on and be ready to call the sheriff's department if we need them. Mike and Bill will stand at the entrance to this trail here and monitor Autumn's progress along the path and into the caves through the camera in her jacket. Erica and I will follow Autumn for as long as she wants or needs us."

"What about me?" Zach asked.

"We'd like you to take this other trail here," Erica said. "According to the map, it's a higher elevation and we're hoping you'll be able to see our lights as we're walking. It eventually meets up with the other path at the cave entrance."

"Okay," Zach agreed. "Autumn, could you please wait until I reach the cave entrance before you go inside?"

"No promises," she said, her eyes shining with excitement. "If I can go in there without being seen, I'll do it."

Zach sighed. This was the same way he had seen her this afternoon, and he briefly wondered if he should change the plan and have Nate and Erica follow the higher path. They had been the ones to invite him along, though, and he decided that he'd simply do his best to reach Autumn in time.

"Let's get going," he suggested. They went out to their cars. Erica and Autumn decided to ride with Zach. As they left the resort, he saw Marvin and Mitzi standing on the porch of the general store. Mitzi was speaking on the phone. Neither of them waved in response to Autumn's raised hand.

Mike followed Zach down the gravel road past Stan's house until they reached the parking lot. Both trail heads had chains across them, but it was easy enough to walk around the barriers. Tiffany settled into the driver's seat of Mike's car as the two cousins set up their computer equipment. Autumn put on her jacket and adjusted the backpack on her shoulders until it rested comfortably against her body.

Nate placed the camera in her pocket. "Got a signal?" he asked Mike in a quiet voice.

"Turn around and let's see if we can view the area," Bill responded.

Autumn turned in a circle. She had stopped smiling and was now focused on what waited for her down the path. "Working?" she asked.

"Yep," Mike said. "We can see everything clearly."

"Okay." Autumn took a deep breath. "Zach, why don't you get a head start down that path?"

He had brought along his own backpack and pulled out a flashlight. Before leaving his cabin, he had placed a knife in the pocket of his jeans, and he patted it reassuringly. "Sure. I'll see you at the cave."

Zach set out on the upper path. Autumn watched him go, suddenly wondering if she should follow him. Nate saw the apprehension on her face and squeezed her arm. "We're ready," he said. "Let's get going."

She nodded. They turned on their lights and set out down the lower path. Although there was still some daylight off to the west, the sun had gone down enough that once they were surrounded by trees they were forced to walk slowly and stay together. "I hope Zach's okay," she whispered as Erica and Nate followed her lead through the forest.

Zach was being followed. He knew that from the sounds in the brush along the trail. Something out there was also breathing heavily from time to time. It wanted him to know he was being watched.

He turned off his light and stood still. Facing down to the lower path, he saw the lights from Nate, Erica, and Autumn moving along at a good pace. Assured that he could reach the cave before them, he kept walking. Halfway down the trail, he heard a growl. He grabbed for his knife and turned around. Nothing was visible, even when he shone his flashlight through the foliage. He transferred the knife to his sweatshirt pocket.

Suddenly, a large rock flew across the pathway in front of him, hit the ground, and went tumbling down the hill. "Nate!" he heard Erica scream. "Autumn, wait!" she yelled an instant later.

Zach trained his attention to the lower path. He could see two flashlights in the middle of the trail and could barely make out Erica standing over Nate. Erica said "I have to go get help! Wait here!"

"Erica? Nate?" Zach called down. He saw them turn to the sound of his voice. "It's Zach. Where's Autumn?"

"She ran off the instant I got hit," Nate called through gritted teeth. "Something just came through here and hit me in the leg."

"I'm on my over," Zach said. He looked around and decided that the quickest way was back through the clearing. When he reached the parking lot, though, he noticed that both cars were gone and so were Tiffany, Mike, and Bill. "What the hell?" he muttered. Starting down the other path, he bumped up his pace to a light jog until he found Nate and Erica.

"Thank God," Erica said. "Can you help me get him out of here?"

"I need to find Autumn," Zach said. "Can't you reach Mike, Bill, or Tiffany?"

Nate, sitting on a nearby stump with a pained expression on his face, shook his head. "The signal sucks out here. Autumn went ahead with the camera."

"Isn't Tiffany supposed to be in the parking lot with her cell phone?"

"She's not there?"

"No. I just came through there. Mike and Bill and Tiffany were gone."

For a moment, they were all quiet. The best chance to get help would be to have Nate and Erica get to Stan's house, but it would be a long walk on an injured leg. He was just about to suggest that the other two wait here when they heard a long, mournful howl coming from somewhere in the forest.

Zach held up a hand as Erica stifled a scream. He took a few steps down the path, put his hands to his mouth, and with a deep breath he gave the fiercest shout he could manage. Even in his pain, he saw that Nate looked impressed. His heart sank as moments passed and there was no response.

Erica dug into her backpack and pulled out the digital recorder. "There's one on here," she hissed. "We had it ready to go for tonight."

Zach took a few deep breaths and nodded. He held it up into the air and pressed the play. The sound that came out was nearly identical to the one they had just heard. "From the other night," Nate said in response to Zach's questioning glance.

This time, they received a response. "It's down the trail," Zach said. "That's where Autumn was going. I'm heading that way too."

They turned as a lantern suddenly switched on. Zach's eyes widened in surprise as he saw George and Reilly. The two men had snuck up on them in the darkness while they had been trying to imitate the Bigfoot. "Having trouble out here?" Reilly asked, immediately focusing on Nate clutching his leg.

"Something threw a rock with so much strength that it passed me, went down the hill, and hit Nate," Zach said. "And Autumn is heading to the cave by herself."

"Let's go," George said. He clutched a rifle. Seeing Zach look at the weapon, he smiled. "Just for protection."

"Did you see our friends?" Erica asked.

"I brought them to my dad's house," George said. He handed Erica the keys to his truck. "Go on and help him out of here. It's not far to the clearing. Then drive up the road a few miles and you'll see my dad waiting for you at his driveway."

"Thank you," Nate said, clenching his teeth. He leaned on Erica, and together they started down the path.

"Now you two head on down to the cave," Reilly said. "I'll stay out here in case something anyone else decides they're crazy enough to come down here."

CHAPTER 17

When Autumn entered the cave, she checked the video recorder. It was on and working. She placed it back it in the clear pocket on the front of her jacket. With the beam of her flashlight trained on the floor and feeling she could use the hefty tool as a weapon, she started to walk slowly through the darkness.

"Autumn." The word was whispered urgently in the still air. Autumn turned around and saw Zach at the entrance to the cave. George was beside him, a rifle ready in his hand. Autumn paused, then turned to the path in front of her and kept going. She could already see the glow of a fire further into the cave.

"Damn," Zach swore. "Let's go in after her."

"I don't think we have a choice," George agreed solemnly. The two men set out into the cave.

Autumn's heart raced as she drew closer to the dim orange glow. She could make out a rounded doorway and stopped to pull her camera out and silently run it through the air to take in the sight. She tucked the camera back in her pocket and turned off the flashlight, but didn't let go of it. She could now see her path.

She peeked around the doorway and had to stifle the scream that almost came out of her. The Bigfoot Stan had injured earlier was sitting in the far corner of a large stone room. It was sitting beside a bloody animal and staring into the flames coming from a large fire pit.

Autumn's hand trembled. She was just about to pull the camera from her pocket when a strong, hairy hand clamped over her mouth and she tried to scream. The hair muffled her voice and she was suddenly swept up into the air.

From several feet away, Zach and George saw the swift attack by the younger creature. George kept his gun level and moved forward. Zach, feeling adrenaline pulse through his veins, ran around the older man. "Autumn!" he shouted, hoping to attract the attention of the beast.

Autumn heard Zach somewhere behind her, but her attention was focused on the Bigfoot. The wounded one struggled to stand up. The Bigfoot who had brought her in dropped her down onto the rocky floor and she felt pain run up and down her arm. He came into her line of sight and she gasped.

This one was even taller than the injured creature, and just as wide. His mouth was set in a grim line, and Autumn was again aware of how eerily human their faces looked. His hair was a darker brown, and she guessed that this was the young Bigfoot that George had mentioned. He looked at the other Bigfoot in the cave and shook his head. As he turned back to Autumn, he let out a howl.

The sound sent shivers through Autumn and made her wince. She brought her arms up to cover her ears, noticing a tear in her sleeve and blood on her left arm. This time the creature growled. "Zach!" Autumn screamed. Suddenly she was afraid that this creature might kill her.

He swung his arm, and she fumbled for her flashlight. Ducking away from his charge at her, she swung the weapon and caught his hand. She heard a large crack and the creature howled again, clutching his hand. He turned his back to her. She knew she only had a moment in which to act, so she brought out her pocket knife and fumbled with it.

The older Bigfoot started to shuffle over to her. She saw him approach and swiped at his arm with the knife. She was close enough to make contact and saw both blood and a small piece of skin on the knife when she drew it away. She tossed the knife into her coat pocket and adrenaline surged through her as the younger one turned back to face her.

Zach appeared at the entrance with George behind him. The younger Bigfoot turned and stomped his feet in the direction of the two men. George walked right up to him, somehow managing to keep the gun level. "Get her out of here," he said to Zach. The Bigfoot, seeming to recognize the weapon, backed up towards the fire pit.

Autumn allowed Zach to help her up. She adjusted her

backpack, which had helped to partially cushion her fall on the rocks. They started towards the outer cave, keeping an eye on the creatures. George backed up with them.

Suddenly, the older Bigfoot roared. He dashed towards Autumn and grabbed at her coat. She screamed and instinctively reached for the camera. It fumbled out of her pocket and landed on the ground. The Bigfoot picked it up, sniffed it, and threw it into the fire.

"No!" Autumn screamed. "We were recording this!"

"Are you fucking insane?" George said, as the beasts moved closer to the humans. "You're alive. That's good enough for now."

They continued to back out. Once they reached the outer cave, Zach turned on his flashlight. "Okay, time to make a run for it," he told Autumn and George. "Ready?"

They nodded. The older Bigfoot appeared in the doorway, seemingly ready to run after them. Autumn didn't hesitate, but took off without the benefit of the flashlight. Zach ran after her. George ran for a few seconds, then turned around.

The two Bigfoot were following them. He recognized the face of the older one, as it had looked into his home many times. "Son of a bitch," he said. "It's time for you to leave me alone."

He pointed the rifle at the cave ceiling and fired two shots. Several rocks poured down, a couple of which hit the older Bigfoot on his bloody arm. He howled.

Zach and Autumn turned around. "George!" Autumn screamed. "George!"

George heard Autumn, but stayed put for a minute longer. He fired one more shot into the ceiling and enough rocks came down to create a small barrier between him and the two monsters. Startled, they backed up until he could only see the reflections of their eyes. "Stay where you belong," he shouted to them, not knowing if they could understand.

He turned and ran, relieved when he finally joined Zach and Autumn at the cave entrance. Autumn hugged him, then shrugged off her backpack and coat as they moved down the trail. "Wait," she told Zach. "I need to put this knife in my bag."

A lantern appeared. Reilly, one hand on his gun, emerged from the darkness. "I heard shots," he told George. "What happened?"

"I managed to get them to back off," he replied. "I guess the falling rocks startled them. They don't want to be stuck in there, unable to get food or water."

"Are you two okay?" Reilly asked Autumn and Zach.

Zach nodded, unable to speak. He didn't know what to make of what he had just seen. The creatures were so eerily similar to humans, yet wild enough that they didn't belong anyplace where humans were living. He was also worried about Autumn, and knew she needed to get her arm looked at.

Autumn, trying to complete her task while avoiding her injured left arm, pulled the knife from her pocket and placed it in a bag and into her back pack. The camera was gone, but hopefully Mike and Bill had managed to keep up the signal until the device had been thrown into the fire.

Reilly swung his lantern around at the approach of rapid footsteps. They all turned in time to see the younger Bigfoot run out from the forest and grab Autumn's backpack and jacket. He ran back down the path, and just beyond the range of the light they saw his shadowy figure smash the bag against a stump as it continued back to the cave.

Zach turned to Autumn. "No," she moaned, slumping to the ground. He eased down to make sure she didn't fall over. "Everything we collected. We're going to look like fools."

"You're alive," Zach whispered to her, and put his arms around her. "Let's worry about all the other stuff in the morning."

Reilly and George waited patiently as Autumn sat quietly for a few moments. There was no other sound around them, which made Zach nervous. He wanted to get out of the area in case there was another Bigfoot they hadn't yet encountered. "Okay, I'm ready," Autumn said. Her phone beeped, and she reached for it. Luckily, she had placed it in the pocket of her sweatshirt instead of her coat.

"The others are asking if we're okay," she told Reilly. "I guess we better get back to them."

He nodded, and motioned for all of them to follow. As they walked, George unloaded his rifle and Reilly placed his gun back into its holster. Zach kept looking around, and Autumn seemed oblivious to anything going on around her. Even when Zach helped her into the sheriff's car, her head hung down and he could see tears falling down her cheeks. They drove down the gravel road in silence until they reached Stan's house.

CHAPTER 18

When Autumn, Zach, Reilly, and George emerged from the car, the other members of the team surrounded them. They had been seated around the fire pit, a strong blaze emitting enough heat and light to ward off any animal that would have wanted to approach. Tiffany looked at Autumn and silently pulled her into a hug. Zach saw Stan in the doorway of his home, shaking his head.

Zach placed his hand on Autumn's shoulder and she turned away, shaking. He saw Tiffany whisper the word "later" and nodded. He left the group and went into Stan's house to talk to George and Stan. Reilly got back into his car to wait for Joey.

Tiffany led her over to the fire. "What happened, Autumn?" Mike asked once they had steered her to a chair near the fire. "We were stationed there at the entrance and Deputy Reilly pulled up to tell us to come back here. We didn't have much of a choice."

"It's okay," she replied in a weak voice. She looked over at Nate. "Are you okay? I'm sorry I just ran down the trail without checking on you"

"Erica and I were just a bit behind you when a large rock came rolling down the hill and hit me." He gestured to his ankle, which had been wrapped in a bandage. "Turns out Stan's other son is a doctor, and he just happened to be here when Erica and I arrived."

"You should have him look at that arm," Erica said. "And you scared us when you ran off to the cave on your own."

Autumn nodded. She looked around at her friends, their faces expecting a story. She took a deep breath and let it out. "I saw two Bigfoot," Autumn said. She felt numb. "Maybe a parent and a grown child. That was the one that probably injured you, Nate. It came up behind me in the cave, picked me up, and dropped me in full view of the other one." She continued to relate the story. Erica wrapped a blanket around her.

"And so all of our proof is gone," she finished. "Ironically stolen by a Bigfoot."

Mike and Bill glanced at each other. "We could try looking for it."

"No!" Autumn shrieked. Her friends all stared at her. "Let's just get out of here and admit defeat this time."

The team sat silently around the fire pit, staring bleakly into the blaze and finishing their drinks. They knew what waited for them when they went back to the city to post their experiences on the BOG forum. They had seen plenty of other people called out to be frauds and liars for posting sightings that seemed unbelievable even to the rest of the people on the forum.

Inside the house, Zach heard Autumn's outburst but turned his attention back to Stan and his sons. "Do you think Autumn is going to have any problems from this?" he asked.

"She did physically attack them," George pointed out. "She lives far enough away that they probably won't find her but she'll be seeing them in her head for a long time."

"That's a brave young woman," Stan admitted. "But her devotion to this cause may have cost her some emotional stability."

Carson stood. Although he had spoken to Reilly for a few minutes after the deputy's arrival, neither man had given a hint as to what they had said. He had been quiet since coming back inside the house. Now, he looked through the open door. "Looks like Joey's here," he said. "I hope nothing else has happened tonight."

Outside, Autumn and her friends watched as Joey pulled her car in next to Reilly. They spoke to each other through the windows, with Joey's gestures clear even to Zach, who had come out onto Stan's porch with the other men. Reilly opened his door, and he and Joey both got out of their cars.

Autumn felt every nerve in her body freeze. She was the only one to hear the first growl from just beyond the woodshed. "Listen!" she shouted. Everyone, including the deputies, turned to her.

"There's something here," she hissed. She somehow found the courage to stand and turn around. There was no clearly defined shape, but she knew that at least one of the Bigfoot had found them.

"Oh my God," George said. He was the first to be at her side. "Now I've brought them here."

"No, I did," Autumn said sadly just before the younger Bigfoot emerged from its hiding spot and howled.

"Holy shit!" Mike and Bill yelled in unison. They immediately moved over to Nate's chair to stand in front of him. Tiffany and Erica joined the group, leaving Autumn and George in front of the Bigfoot.

Zach saw this and stepped off the porch. "Be careful what you do," Stan hissed. Carson stayed silent.

Reilly and Joey approached with their guns drawn. They now had the only weapons in reach with the exception of the axe just a few feet away from Zach. He stared at it, and looked at the Bigfoot's position in front of him.

The animal raised its arm and pointed straight at Autumn. She shuddered. "No."

In disbelief, she watched as the creature nodded its head. It took two steps forward, and turned its head to look at her friends. They were all frozen in place, not willing to make a move for any cameras or phones. She saw Tiffany collapse, but Bill caught her and held her in place next to Nate.

It pointed at her again. "No," Zach said. He had come up from behind the creature. The Bigfoot turned to Zach as he swung the axe.

He missed on the first attempt. The creature swung out its arm and hit Zach across the chest. He felt pressure and pain as he was knocked to the ground and rolled over. The axe dropped from his hands, but he reached out to grab it. His chest burned with every move as he rose, and heard Autumn scream his name. The adrenaline helped him as he rushed toward the Bigfoot and swung the axe again.

This time it connected with flesh. The creature's injured hand was thrown against a tree. The desperate combination of sounds that emerged from the monster made Zach's blood freeze. Without thinking, he instantly drew his arm back and swung again.

The Bigfoot's hairy hand dropped to the ground next to the woodshed. The creature screamed and grasped its arm. Blood dripped down to the ground, and Zach felt himself grow weak. Stan caught him just as he fell to the ground, unable to make his mind truly comprehend that he had just cut off the hand of a Bigfoot.

The creature glared at them all and disappeared into the night. Silence fell over the crowd. "Oh my god," Joey said. "Reilly, did that just actually happen?"

"I warned you about that," he told her. He gave a slight nod to Carson, and the doctor quietly went to work. Stan pulled Zach up from the ground and walked him over to join the others at the fire pit. Reilly and Joey stood next to them, their bodies seeming to form a shield against the activity behind them at the woodshed.

"Okay, folks, I think it's time you all headed back to your campsites for the evening," he said. "Hopefully by daylight this will all seem like a bad dream."

"Not likely," Autumn muttered. She reached out for Zach's hand. They now shared a connection they hadn't had before. She could see in his eyes that he was still trying to make sense of the evening.

"Still, I think we should all clear out of here. Obviously, these creatures have been disturbed and would prefer to not have us in their territory."

"Tell me one thing," Zach demanded, his head suddenly clear. "Are the people in town hiding something about Bigfoot?"

"It's not really hiding so much as protecting," Stan admitted. George and Reilly glared at him. He shrugged. "It's the truth."

"Come on, folks," Joey said. "I'll escort those of you at the campground back to your site."

"We're sleeping in the RV with you and Nate tonight,"

Mike warned Tiffany.

"Of course," she agreed. They hobbled and walked to the car and Joey followed them back out onto the road.

While Zach prepared to leave, he saw Autumn wander over to the woodshed. Carson had disappeared into the house. "The hand," she whispered to him.

"What?' he whispered back.

"Where's the hand? It should have fallen around here."

Zach looked around and saw nothing on the ground. He looked closer in the leftover light from the fire and saw that the ground appeared to have been raked. "Someone disposed of it for us," he said, his voice turning bitter. "How nice of them."

He put an arm around her and motioned for Erica to follow them. Reilly, George, Stan, and Carson all gathered around the fire pit as the others left. Once Zach's car was out of sight, the men let out a collective sigh.

"For the vault," Carson said as he handed a tightly wrapped group of towels to Reilly. The hand was inside, along with some dirt from around the shed.

"Some day I have to see this vault," Stan chuckled. "You ever think we should have everything in there examined?"

"Can you imagine the crowds of people coming through here if scientists determined that an unknown species was living here?" Reilly demanded. "No. This gets passed down to the next set of deputies through here, but that's all."

"I'm going to the shelter in the morning" Carson said. "I bet Zach is going to be looking for answers."

"I'll come along," Reilly replied.

"Good." Carson stood up. "In the meantime, it's late, and I think most of the action for tonight is over."

"Yep," George agreed. "Maybe they'll even leave me alone for a while."

Carson looked at his brother with sympathy. He knew how hard Harry's death must have been to witness, since he had been one of the men to go down and retrieve the body. George had not listened to warnings about staying away from the cave, and it had cost him a lot in life. He hoped that the young woman, Autumn, would have better luck.

Everyone left. Stan, finally alone, sat next to the fire pit to think about the Bigfoot down in the cave. He knew that he was the closest residence to them, and yet they had never bothered him unless someone else was here. Tahoma Valley should be quiet now for some time, unless the creatures decided to venture out closer to humans later in the summer. Sometimes they did that. Sometimes people went missing. He tried hard not to think about it.

A rustling in the bushes across the driveway caught his attention. Startled, he sat up and stared at the leaves. To his relief, a raccoon emerged from the foliage and wandered down the driveway. Satisfied, Stan put out the fire. Just as he started to his front door, he paused and turned around.

There was enough moonlight to allow him to see as far as the road. Just beyond the light, a tall shadow waited. "Go away," he said quietly, and then ran into his house. He pulled down all the shades, turned off the lights, and locked himself into the bedroom. He had had enough excitement for tonight. He'd wait for tomorrow and hope that nothing outside tried to come into his home while he was sleeping.

CHAPTER 19

When Zach woke up on Sunday morning, his whole body ached. He took a couple of pills for the pain and stiffness, then slowly got out of bed. The sun was already shining over the trees. A glance out the window showed him some movement across the creek, around the shelter.

He walked slowly down the stairs and put on his shoes. He had fallen into bed with his sweatpants and t-shirt, so he simply pulled on his hooded sweatshirt and went to investigate. He walked around the cabin. When he reached the edge of the creek, he stopped to take in what was happening around the structure.

Two men were quietly walking in and out of the shelter. Carson and Reilly were saying very little to each other. Zach figured they didn't want to catch the attention of anyone else who might be staying in the cabins. They were intent on their work and didn't notice Zach. He didn't try to get their attention.

He felt someone come up beside him and turned around, startled. Autumn stared across the creek. She watched the two men as they appeared to be cleaning up whatever Bigfoot might have left behind. Every now and then they looked in the direction of the tree stand that they had explored yesterday. "I wonder if they're trying to avoid us or Bigfoot," Autumn murmured.

"So, the local people try to draw people's attention away from where Bigfoot actually lives." He nodded his head at the men when they finally turned around at the sound of his voice. "Autumn. How are you feeling today?"

"Sore. Disappointed. Bitter at losing all my evidence."

"I think I still have some pictures," Zach said. "When are you and Erica leaving?"

"Erica just got up. We're going to meet the others at campground around noon, and probably decide what to do from there. We have the cabin for another hour, so we'll be here until then." She looked across the creek again. "Do you really think those Bigfoot come to that shelter?"

"Yes. When it's dark, most likely. I think we now know that they're not all that interested in dealing with humans." He turned back to the cabin. "I need to take a shower and pack. Please come over before you leave."

"Okay." Autumn turned away, her body moving stiffly. She wandered back over to her cabin, and Zach watched to make sure she closed the door behind her before going to his car and retrieving his backpack. When he opened the door, he realized with a sinking feeling that he had forgotten to lock the car.

He hurried inside and turned on the camera. Sure enough, when he tried to go back and retrieve all the pictures he had taken that weekend, including the ones of the shelter, they had all been erased. "Damn," he said softly under his breath. He guessed that George or one of his friends had come by last night hoping to be able to destroy any remaining evidence. He wondered if they would have smashed his car window in, and figured that they might have and simply blamed it on the monster if questioned about it.

He looked around in his backpack and discovered a note tucked in the front pocket. "Dear Zach," he read out loud. "I'm sorry about the camera, but we really don't want more people to get hurt. I hope you return to Tahoma Valley sometime in the future. Thank you. Reilly."

He folded the note and placed it back into the bag. The police officer had come to his car and erased the evidence of Bigfoot he was carrying. He dug into the bag. His hand hit on one plastic vial, and he brought it out.

Reilly had left the hair sample. Either he had not noticed it, which Zach found unlikely, or else he knew that scientists couldn't determine anything from it. Zach vowed to send it somewhere to be analyzed. While the show had an agreement with a lab in New York, Zach decided to keep his evidence local and find a place near here that would take care of it.

The BOG members really had been through their own creature hunt. They had set out to prove the existence of

Bigfoot, and while very little physical evidence had survived the weekend, they did have their own stories and recollections. Thinking of that, he went back outside and found Reilly and Carson sitting on rocks near the creek behind his cabin. "I'm guessing you found your camera?" Reilly asked.

"Yes. Is there anything else you want to confess to taking?"

"Not from you." The sheriff's deputy stretched his arms. "Look, we can get back to normal in Tahoma Valley this week. The Bigfoot aren't going to want to engage with humans after what happened to them last night."

"I hope you understand how serious we are about this," Carson added. "We want them to be left alone."

Zach looked over at the shelter. "Someone else is going to see that in the next few days."

Carson shrugged. "Let them. The previous ones that were built didn't seem to be a problem except to anyone interested in Bigfoot."

Zach understood that. To anyone who didn't have knowledge or interest in cryptozoology, it would just look like a cool shelter put together for kids to play in. Hopefully parents would either keep the kids away or keep them supervised. Either way, they wouldn't question its presence or what purpose it served.

"Mitzi mentioned more than one previous shelter," he remembered.

"Several have been built over the years," Carson said. "Sometimes we take them down, sometimes the weather and elements do the job for us."

Zach nodded. "Maybe I'll see you two in the future," he said. The men rose and he shook their hands.

"Have a nice summer, Zach. Maybe I'll tune into your show from time to time," Reilly said with a wink. He and Carson crossed the creek and disappeared down the path beyond it.

Zach ran back into the cabin. He made sure the door was

locked and went upstairs to take a shower. After he was done, he dressed and packed all his clothing. Mitzi had told him that the linens would be changed, so he didn't even make an effort to straighten the sheets or comforter. Realizing he was hungry, he brought everything downstairs and made coffee while putting breakfast together. He sat at the kitchen table to eat and through the front window saw Erica leaving Cabin 2 and heading in the direction of the general store.

After Erica returned from the store with drinks for the ride home, Autumn piled their luggage into the car and slammed the trunk. "We're not leaving yet, are we?" Erica asked when Autumn returned to the living room.

"No, we still have some time." Autumn looked through the bag of groceries on the table. She was in pain, although the pills she had taken that morning were starting to work. Her emotions were up and down. She knew that the giant chocolate bar she was now unwrapping wasn't going to do much for her, but she wanted it anyway.

Erica took a sip of coffee and looked at her with concern. "Maybe you should see a doctor," she said. "Where do you hurt?"

"Mostly my arm. It's scratched and bruised, but I don't think it's too bad. My pride hurts more than anything."

Erica hugged her. "Autumn, take care of yourself."

"I'm trying," Autumn said, and her voice unexpectedly gave way to a whimper. She dropped the candy and slid down onto the couch. She then surprised herself by sobbing uncontrollably for nearly ten minutes while Erica sat next to her silently.

Autumn finally took some deep breaths to calm herself down. She realized that her head was clear. "I guess I needed that," she said to Erica. Her friend nodded and rubbed her arm.

"Yeah, I think you did."

"Weren't you scared last night?"

"I cried in the shower," Erica admitted. "I don't think you

heard me."

"No," Autumn admitted. She frowned at the chocolate on the floor. "Well, that's done."

After she threw away the candy, she and Erica finished their coffee, washed the dishes, and left the cabin. "I'll go check out if you want to say goodbye to Zach," Erica said with a wink.

Autumn blushed. "Okay." She walked over to Cabin 1 and knocked on the door.

Zach opened it and smiled. "Hey, come in," he offered, pushing aside a duffel bag on the living room floor.

"I can't stay long because Erica is checking out. I just wanted to thank you for joining us this weekend."

Zach smiled again and her heart raced. "You're welcome."

"Thank you for saving my life," Autumn added. She felt like she was going to cry again. "I mean that. I know you took a lot of risks down at the cave and Stan's house."

"Some of that was to save my own life," Zach pointed out softly. He rubbed his chest. "You're welcome, Autumn. I'm glad I was here this weekend to save you from Bigfoot."

"I bet you say that to all the women," Autumn replied.

They both laughed. "Where are you going from here?" Autumn asked.

"Home, probably for a couple of months. I don't start filming shows again until the producers decide what to investigate. How about you?"

"Back to my boring life as a library assistant and cat parent." She smiled. "Home sounds good right now."

"It does," Zach agreed. He went over to the table and picked up a business card. "Please feel free to contact me, Autumn. I'd like to hear more about your experiences with the BOG forum."

"I'll be watching your show," Autumn promised. "Stay safe out there, Zach."

He pulled her into a hug and she let herself relax in his arms. She tried to not press on his chest, but placed her head on his shoulder. When he gently let her go, she longed to ask him to hold her again.

He surprised her by giving her a soft quick kiss. "Erica is waiting by the car," he whispered.

"Darn," Autumn replied. He opened the front door and squeezed her hand, then led her outside.

"Bye, Autumn."

"Bye, Zach."

She turned and walked to the car. Erica waved at Zach and got into the passenger seat. "Everything okay?" she asked.

"Everything's great," Autumn replied.

CHAPTER 20

When they arrived at the campground, it was bustling with people taking down tents and packing coolers. Nate was sitting in the front seat of the RV, able to drive because it was his left leg that was injured. Tiffany had just finished packing everything away into storage bins. Mike and Bill had taken down their tent and were two talking to two men who looked familiar.

"Aren't those the guys who were with Tony?" Erica asked.

"I think so," Autumn said, her good mood starting to fade. She parked and nodded at the men as she and Erica got out of the car. "Hi, Mike. Hi, Bill."

"Hi, Autumn," they chorused. Nate got up from his seat and limped to the doorway. Tiffany helped him get down from the vehicle.

"This is Aaron and Cal," Bill told Autumn and Erica. "They're on a team with Tony Simons."

"We know he wasn't very nice to you the other day," Cal said. "We just wanted to let you all know that he's decided to take some time away from the forum."

"We heard he was injured," Nate said with a question in his voice.

"Yeah. He got knocked on the head by something," Aaron replied. "In the woods up by the Valley Tavern on Friday night."

"We dropped by there Thursday night and a sheriff's deputy tried to steer us away from some caves that were on an old map," Cal added.

The team looked at each other. "Really," Mike said in a flat tone.

"Yep. We were going to go out there yesterday but didn't want to explore without Tony." Aaron stretched. "There sure wasn't any activity out on the other side of town last night. You all see anything?"

"Nothing we can prove," Autumn laughed. "You know

how that goes."

"Sure do," Cal said. "Have a good day."

They left. Autumn and her friends looked at each other. "So, Tony gets hit on the head by something and that keeps him away from us on the biggest night of the hunt," Tiffany said. "I'm not sure what to say."

"I'd say thank you to Bigfoot," Autumn replied.

After saying goodbye to Autumn, Zach checked out of the resort. "Hope you enjoyed your stay," Mitzi said, smiling.

"Did you hear about last night?" he asked casually.

Her smile faded, but she remained friendly. "Yes. It's too bad that some people got hurt."

"Have you seen one of the Bigfoot?" Zach asked.

He saw a family in a minivan pull up in front of the office, ready to check out. Mitzi greeted the husband and took care of his payment, then waited until he left the office before answering Zach. "I'm not sure. I've seen tall shadowy figures and heard things following me in the woods. But that doesn't stop me from aiding those who have seen it in protecting the Bigfoot from outsiders."

Zach nodded. "I understand."

"You do?"

"Autumn and I saw Carson and Reilly looking over that branch shelter across the creek this morning. I'm guessing you probably call them when something gets left behind so they can collect it and place it wherever they keep all the rest of the evidence they've taken."

"Then you know that we just want the creature to be left alone. It's caused enough grief around here."

"I can't guarantee that people aren't going to come here. Autumn and her friends will surely spread the story of their encounters."

Mitzi shook her head. "That's too bad."

"I like this place, Mitzi. I'm coming back here sometime for an actual vacation."

Her smile appeared again. "We'd be glad to have you."

Zach stopped at the general store to look around one more time. He found a plush Bigfoot wearing a black shirt with "Tahoma Valley" written on the front. Remembering Brandon's joke about bringing him back a Bigfoot, Zach purchased it. The cameraman would get a good laugh out of it the next time they saw each other.

Zach returned to his car and drove to the entrance of the resort. He paused. He had two options. He could go straight home. Or, he could go back down to the cave and see if there was anything else to be found.

He knew Autumn and Erica had gone to the campground to meet with their friends before going home. Maybe there was a chance that he could recover the stolen backpack and let Autumn know he had her evidence. He tried to tell himself that the area would be safer in the daylight, and that he'd be able to see or hear anything approaching him.

"Damn it," he muttered. Before this weekend, he would never have considered doing something like this. Autumn and her friends seemed to have passed on their enthusiasm about Bigfoot to him.

"I'll do it." He turned left and sped down the road. Several cars passed him going the other way. Families were coming to the mountain for day trips and picnics, unaware of what lurked in the forest around them.

He reached Forest Hill Road and slowly pulled off the highway. He passed Stan's house and the bruise across his chest seemed to send painful signals to his brain. He still couldn't wrap his mind around the fact that a Bigfoot had hit him. He imagined Autumn felt the same way about her physical encounters in the cave.

Stan wasn't in sight, and Zach didn't want to stop and chat with him. He had a mission down here. He reached the parking lot and left his car in the shade near the entrance to the upper path. The lower path looked ominous even at this time of day, so he picked up his flashlight to use as a weapon and set out on his walk.

His body started to send him warnings as he progressed

down the path. He felt something watching him, but when he stopped every few minutes there were no sounds coming from the surrounding woods. When he reached the spot where Autumn's backpack had been taken, he slowed down and strolled along the side of the path, hoping to find it somewhere in the brush on the hillside. Every dark patch raised his interest, but when he tried to get closer each time, he discovered it was just a trick of his eyes.

He didn't notice that he had reached the cave until he took his eyes away from the forest. He stopped, listening for footsteps and watching for movement. The instant he took a step in the direction of the cave, he heard a low growl coming from somewhere off to his right, on the opposite side of the trail.

He stopped and listened. Tree branches rustled halfway up the hillside, but he couldn't see anything. He turned on the flashlight and pointed it at the cave. Instantly, he saw the reflector patch on the backpack. It was right inside the entrance. He strained to look at it and saw that it had been ripped apart, but light reflected off of plastic containers sitting on the ground beside it.

Zach looked around nervously. He still sensed that Bigfoot was nearby, watching him. He felt this was a trap, but his experience told him that he still needed to try to retrieve the evidence. He stepped forward, shuffling closer to the cave.

The backpack was now clearly in sight, close enough that he could quickly grab it and run. His flashlight played over the rest of the cave, and he shuddered when two eyes reflected back at him. Another growl came from the hillside, echoed by one coming from inside the cave.

Zach's heart was racing. "Okay," he said clearly. He turned off the flashlight. "Okay. It belongs to you." He backed away from the cave, now able to hear footsteps up on the hill moving through the bushes

He dug into his pocket and the found the vial of hair. Without the rest of the evidence, it would mean nothing. He tossed it carefully into the cave, where it landed on the backpack. A soft whoop came from the forest, and Zach sighed in defeat.

"Goodbye," he whispered, turning away from the cave with regret. He walked away with long strides, showing the Bigfoot that he was leaving. About halfway to the parking lot, he finally heard the footsteps subside and decided that the creature following him had decided he was no longer a threat.

He reached the parking lot and breathed a long sigh of relief. Stan must have seen him drive by, because he was now standing beside Zach's car. "Find what you were looking for?" he asked casually.

"Look, I didn't just come here on a whim. I thought I could try to find Autumn's backpack and maybe salvage some of the hair and blood samples and photos that she and the others gathered this weekend."

"Zach, I like you. And it's because I like you that I'm asking you to please just go home and leave Bigfoot alone." Stan sighed. "Christ, didn't last night teach you anything? They're monsters, wild animals beyond our control."

"My job is to look for creatures like Bigfoot," Zach argued. "Before I joined the show, I'll admit to probably being one of the biggest skeptics out there. Hell, I even get tired sometimes of being out in the forest in the middle night with people who think every shake of a tree limb is something coming for them. But at the heart of it all I've come to believe in cryptids, and I want people who share that belief to know they're not crazy."

Stan's face was sympathetic. "We have a long tradition here of keeping Bigfoot a secret from the public. You know what you experienced. We can't stop you from talking about it, but you and the BOG people aren't going to get any verbal or physical support from us."

"I understand," Zach said wearily. He turned around. The trailhead was empty and suddenly the forest had lost its allure. "I think I'll go home now. I still have some time before the show starts again to think through what happened here."

"Good luck." Stan stepped aside as Zach got into his car. He waved as the younger man drove out the parking lot, slowly scanning the bushes at the side of the road.

Stan heard rustling behind him. A long, hairy arm reached out from the foliage and dropped a black backpack onto the ground. When Zach had gone to the cave this morning, they had probably guessed what he was looking for.

The arm pulled back and Stan heard heavy breathing and a growl. He knew what those noises meant. He picked up the bag to give to Carson and Reilly later, then walked quickly out of the parking lot. He did not turn around to see the two Bigfoot briefly emerge from the forest, look at each other, and then disappear back into the trees.

CHAPTER 21

When Autumn pulled into her driveway late Sunday afternoon, she turned off the car engine and sat quietly for several moments before getting out. Neighborhood kids were still out running around on their lawns, and their parents were chatting with each other in a couple of groups. She had a moment where she realized that she didn't really know most of her neighbors and wondered what they thought of her.

Realizing some of them were probably looking her way, she got out of the car and pulled her bags from the back seat. She knew she looked tired and dirty, despite the shower this morning. It seemed like the dust from the roads in Tahoma Valley had followed her home. Her favorite sweatshirt was covered in dirt from their search on Friday morning, when she had slipped and fallen. She walked to the front door with her head down.

She had barely closed and locked the door when tears welled up in her eyes and fell furiously down her face. She sank to the floor beside the couch and sobbed for at least fifteen minutes, every now and then looking up through the window to make sure no one saw her. Finally, she weakly pulled herself up onto the couch and smiled as Squatch came walking into the room, curious about his owner's behavior.

"Hi, Squatch," she whispered, petting his fur. He purred and nudged her face, licked at her tears, and then smelled her shirt. He backed off to the other end of the couch, but curled up and kept his eyes on her.

"Do I smell like another animal?" she asked the cat. "I probably do. I was out in the woods this weekend."

Squatch blinked, and Autumn smiled again. Her muscles were starting to ache again, but there was something she needed to take care of online before she took care of herself. She sat down at her computer, turned it on, and impatiently logged in to the BOG forum.

Thoughts swirled through her head. Where to start? What to say? Should she mention Zach? What about Stan and

George?

Finally, she started to type. A matter-of-fact account of the weekend started to form. She and her friends had gone to Tahoma Valley to meet up with others from the forum and find Bigfoot. They had looked in several areas where sightings had been documented and found nothing. On their own, her group had encountered a branch structure and talked to someone in Tahoma Valley who claimed to have had an up-close encounter with Bigfoot, one in which a friend of his was killed.

When she got to the events of the previous night, she paused. Even for the like-minded people on this board, their encounter might be considered an over-the-top exaggeration. Still, she wanted to get it out while her memory of it was fresh. There was precious little evidence left to prove what had happened, and this post would serve as a good reminder for her.

She explained about their trip down to the caves and how she had eventually ended up going inside. She referred to Zach as "a skeptical man from the cabin next to ours who agreed to join us in our investigation" and credited him with helping her escape. She explained that the younger Bigfoot had stolen their evidence. She wrote about how the people of Tahoma Valley knew about Bigfoot and did their best to steer people away from finding it.

Once she was finished writing, she took her hands away from the keyboard before pushing the button that would publish the post. She felt something inside her brain telling her not to tell the story of Bigfoot and her encounter with the creature. She turned back to her computer. Taking a deep breath, she pushed "publish" and sighed as she saw her post go live in the forum.

"Sometimes you have to take a chance," she told Squatch. The cat stared at her.

She pushed away from the computer and ordered a pizza, then used the time before it was delivered to take another shower and put on some clean sweatpants and a t-shirt. When she came back downstairs after unpacking everything from the weekend, it was only a couple of minutes before her dinner arrived.

Taking a few slices of pepperoni pizza and a diet soda with her to the computer, she opened up the forum and saw that more than one hundred comments had already popped up. There were some screen names she recognized and many others that she didn't. Nate and Erica had both logged in to say that they had been with her and her account was accurate. Others said that she was making up her story and that since no one else had been able to find Bigfoot, there was no way her team could have done so. Some of them called her names and told her to get back on whatever medication she had been taking. Others conveyed the same message in a gentler tone, implying that she was hallucinating and maybe needed to take a break from the boards.

She was done crying, so all she could do was smile at some of the messages. No doubt she'd be having some of the same thoughts as most of these posters if she hadn't lived through the most frightening night of her life. She shrugged and decided that maybe some of them were right. She still believed in cryptids, but maybe it was time to take a short break from BOG and other forums. She had enjoyed getting out into the forest this weekend before seeing Bigfoot, and she realized that it was something she wanted to do more of in the future.

Before logging off to finish her dinner in front of the television one more reply to her post appeared. She opened it and flushed with pleasure at the three words in front of her. "I believe you."

A star next to the screen name indicated the user was new to the site. She blinked and read the name again. "ZachLinWA." If she was right, Zach had just given her some quiet support online. She knew that for the sake of his show he probably didn't want to say too much on message boards like these, but knowing that he was out there was enough to give her some comfort.

She turned off the computer, pulled the living room curtains closed, and sank down on the couch. She flipped through the channels, finally settling on more re-runs of *Creature Hunt* and comparing the television version of Zach to the real one. She decided that she liked the real man much better, but his professional demeanor on the show even in the face of some obviously made-up encounters still impressed her. She wondered when new episodes of the show would be filmed.

During a commercial break, she stood up to refill her drink and find some dessert. Squatch was sitting in the kitchen doorway, staring into the empty room. Concerned, she went over and scratched his head. "What's out there?" she asked.

She looked up. The kitchen light was off but the streetlights outside were bright enough to illuminate the large shape looking in through the kitchen window. The ape-like face stared at her, then turned and walked away.

Autumn screamed. She remembered George's story about occasionally seeing a Bigfoot in his window and Stan's conclusion that George was afraid to move because Bigfoot might follow him. She had entered their private domain and taken their blood, and suddenly she realized that she would be the one to pay for it.

"What did I do?" she whispered. She ran back into the living room and huddled under her blanket. She closed her eyes as the episode ended. "What monsters will we look for next? Come join us next week on our creature hunt."

CHAPTER 22

When Zach let himself into his house early Sunday evening, he was still trying to sort out his feelings. There was excitement that he had encountered Bigfoot, dismay that the many of the local people had conspired to keep the events a secret, and loneliness after leaving Autumn.

"I'll call her soon," he decided. She had been brave and adventurous, and also very endearing in the moments they had been alone. Perhaps she would be interested in coming along with him on one of his future quests.

He logged on to his laptop and went upstairs to unpack. When the dirty clothes had been tossed into the washer, he settled down at his computer with a beer and decided to look up the BOG website. As he browsed through it, he was surprised that he had never visited this site before. He had heard other witnesses talking about it, and the sightings were organized by regions all around the country. In fact, he recognized pictures from a branch structure he had seen in Ohio during the first season of filming.

An article posted just a couple of hours ago caught his eye. The title "BOG experiences at Mount Rainier" caught his eye and he opened up. He saw that Autumn had written it and he immediately started reading.

Twenty minutes later, Zach sat back in his chair. She had described their experiences with wonderful detail. Several people responding to the article were already expressing doubts about the encounters in the cave. For people dedicated to finding Bigfoot, Zach thought some of the comments were rather cruel. He wondered if he should lend his support to Autumn through the online forum.

He knew he needed to be cautious about what he wrote on internet forums. If the people knew that the host of the most popular television show about cryptozoology had been with Autumn during the events she related, it would look like they had planned some sort of hoax. He created a user name for the site and thought about what he could write.

He finally decided to keep it simple and hope that other people shared his sentiment. "I believe you," he said out loud as he typed. He was sure that Nate, Tiffany, Erica, Mike, and Bill would chime in. The more people who wrote about it, the more Autumn's story had the possibility of being believed even without photos, videos, or recordings.

He picked up the phone and called Brandon. "Hey, you'll never guess what kind of weekend I had," he said when the cameraman answered. "I ended up going on a Bigfoot hunt after all."

"Really?" Brandon's voice was both amused and skeptical. Zach tried to sum up the adventures of the weekend. Even as he spoke, he knew how crazy it sounded. Maybe this was how Autumn and her friends knew they were viewed in most social circles.

"Wow," Brandon said when the Zach finished his story. "You really did see Bigfoot."

"Yes. I saw it."

"Still a skeptic, after all of that?"

"About some cryptids, yeah. I guess I am."

"Still the same Zach." Brandon chuckled. "Well, you're back just in time. The producers e-mailed us a list of places we're going to investigate for the new season We'll start heading out on the road in August."

Zach sat down on the couch and smiled out the window. "Where are we going?"

"Florida, Arkansas, and northern Minnesota stand out. But we're also returning to New Jersey."

"What?" Zach's voice was sharp.

"I know, but the producers convinced me we should go when they showed me the information they had been getting. It's all focused around a small town called West Pine. It's up in the northern part of the state, far from the usual monster sightings. Apparently, there are reports of more than one cryptid in the area going back for years. The Jersey Devil. Bigfoot. Even some supposed werewolf sightings."

"Okay, just a minute." Keeping Brandon on the line, Zach

went to his computer and ran a search for West Pine. The number of hits that came up piqued his curiosity.

"Sounds interesting," Zach said. "I wonder what new surprises we'll find for the show."

Brandon and Zach chatted for several more minutes, and when Zach finally hung up the phone he was energized again. He'd meet with the producers next month in New York, and then they'd all meet up again in Florida in August to hunt down their version of Bigfoot. The prospect of going out again was exciting, and he wondered if Autumn would feel the same way about her next investigation.

His stomach rumbled, and he decided to go pick up some teriyaki chicken. There was a restaurant just a few blocks away, across from the coffee shop where he had been right before deciding to head out to Mount Rainier. He could walk there and back and then still watch part of the Sunday night baseball game.

When Zach arrived at the restaurant, the smell of the food prompted him to order enough food to have leftovers for a couple of days. He paid for it and sat down at a table to wait for his order. He heard two men talking in a booth a few feet away.

"I heard on the news that a bunch of fools were out near Tahoma Valley this weekend looking for Bigfoot," one man said. "Big surprise, they didn't find anything."

"There's no such thing as Bigfoot," the other man replied.

Zach smiled.

ABOUT THE AUTHOR

C.E. Osborn grew up in Tacoma, Washington, and currently resides in New Jersey. She is a cataloging librarian and an avid reader of mystery and horror novels. You can reach C.E. at www.ceosborn.wordpress.com.

Works by C.E. Osborn

Creature Hunt
Circle of Darkness
Shadow in the Trees
Camp Thunder Cloud

Poetry:
Dream Softly
Before You Take My Hand

Lonely Hollow series:
Lonely Hollow

Printed in Great Britain
by Amazon